The Dragons

of

Dunkirk

a fantasy novel by

Damon Alan

For 30 years I ran role playing games as a game master. Be it 2nd Edition AD&D or West End Games D6 Star Wars, I loved creating stories for my players, and even more when we created a spectacular story as a team. Now that I'm older it's harder to get a group together, but my interest in telling stories never waned. So, I became an author. As some of you know, I have authored several space opera books. That scratches the desire to run a sci-fi game. Here, finally, I am satisfying the passion I have for fantasy worlds. As a bonus, I am adding in WWII elements, a period in our history that fascinates me.

I dedicate this book to all the creators of worlds more fantastic than ours, all the creators of stories for their game playing friends, and all those who came before me in writing about dragons, dwarves, elves, and other fantastical creatures. Tolkien laid a solid and grand foundation for us to build on, a foundation he built from the stones of our mythology. The imagination of the human race is limitless. Embrace it. Dive into other worlds and discover greatness.

This is a work of fiction, and any names, places, characters or events are created solely from the mind of Damon Alan, and then revealed via this book to you, the reader. Any resemblance to any human of the estimated 100 billion humans who live or ever have lived is purely coincidental.

1st Edition E-book, distribution solely via Amazon Kindle Direct Publishing.

1st Edition print book is available on Amazon.com via Createspace as printer.

Contents

Chapter 1 - Calling

Four years before the Joining of Worlds

Irsu hammered his chisel into stone. The granite heart of Iron Mountain was slowly yielding the hearth he'd need to attract a mate. His mother, Selydna, had given him a thousand cubic *horats* of the mountain interior for him to shape his house from.

With the caveat that any gems he found were hers.

And damn her contractual wisdom if he hadn't uncovered some beryl, a host of rose quartz, and three brilliant topaz's that would have bought him ten thousand cubic *horats* elsewhere to call his own if he was able to keep them.

But, if life had taught him one thing, it was not to cheat one's own mother.

He chuckled to think of how she'd tricked him into mining this area for her. A moment of levity, then he returned to shaping the coal bin he'd need to work his forge. The bin was a hole in the floor, with a raised lip to keep any future youngsters from falling into it. Eventually he'd fashion a mushwood lid to separate the dark and dirty fuel from the rest of the hearth.

As the chisel sank into the granite a sliver at a time, he thought of the dust on his face.

Granite dust.

Once this place was finished, the only dust in the four rooms he'd hollowed out would be the coal, as he'd also need fuel to fire the stove if he ever found the wife. Until then it was easier to eat hard bread and dried meat.

"Quit the daydreaming, Irsu," he muttered to himself. "You got a long way to chisel before the ladies will look at this hearth with a covetous heart."

"You Irsu Crackstone?" someone said behind him.

Startled, he hit his head on the edge of the bin and his eyes flashed with the sparkling lights of a hard impact. Then another impact followed, this time his body on the floor of the bin. He'd fallen in. To make matters worse, it was deeper into the floor than he was tall.

"Oooo, that had to hurt!" the voice that startled him said.

Irsu looked up. A young dwarven woman dressed in fine court leather looked down into the bin at his pathetic state.

"Sorry," she said. "I didn't mean to startle you."

"You did a good job considering you did it by accident," he grumbled.

After disappearing and laughing heartily at him for a good minute, she reappeared over the lip of the hole. "I'll help you out," she offered, extending a hand down to him.

For a court woman, she had a fine grip. Strong, like she'd hefted a hammer more than once in her life. Irsu grunted as he slid over the edge onto the floor.

"Help you the rest of the way?" she asked, offering her hand again.

"I got it," he said, his ego throbbing. Had she been a thief, he'd have been locked away helpless while she pillaged his home. Not that there was much even a thief would want. His axe and his armor were his only possessions of noticeable value, and he kept those at Mother's hearth until his was secure. To him they were purely decorative items he'd acquired because any hearth master of quality had the physical means to defend his territory.

But they were still valuable.

"Suit yourself," she said as she unrolled a scroll. "Irsu Crackstone, you are hereby summoned to an audience with the Underking, His Majesty Scorriss Bloodstone."

"What?" Irsu asked.

"Was I not speaking clearly?" she asked. "Or did you hit your head too hard?"

"When?" he asked, hoping his second question would be more to her liking. She was quite fetching now that he got a good look. Full beard, round nose, round hips…

"You're full of queries, aren't you?"

"As are you, lady, read the rest."

"Immediately," she said, and rolled up the scroll. "Also, my eyes are up here."

"I wasn't looking at anything! And why'd you roll the scroll up if you're going to read the rest immediately."

She laughed again. "You're funny! No, coal bin diver, you're to report to the king now, which is what immediately means."

"Couldn't you have read that part with the rest?"

"Yes," she confessed. "You're to return with me. Get ready."

He breathed deep. Patience was running short for the day, he'd already hit two fingers with a hammer and found deepworms in his bread supply. He'd have to buy more bread if he didn't want to reduce his diet to nothing but dried lizard meat, and his purse was looking a bit light these days.

"Lady, I've been working all day. I'm not clean. I tore my best shirt. I haven't had a good meal in a week. And you want me to see King Bloodstone immediately?"

"His words," she said. "Bring that kid even if he looks like a dung beetle's rejected dinner."

Irsu laughed. He probably did look like that, but the King's way of putting situations in common words for the citizens of Iron Mountain clan was one of the reasons he was loved.

He was the Underking, and while his ancestors once ruled several holds such as this one, it was a sad fact that now his people only numbered about twelve thousand, all in one hold. King Bloodstone took the time to know something about each of the families that lived in the mountain.

"He knows I'm working to increase the size of his community and he summons me immediately," Irsu complained. "Considerate."

"Kings don't have to be considerate," the courier replied. "Wash up at least, I'll give you that. We have an excuse for taking so long, what with you falling down the pit like that."

"You can't tell him that!" Irsu exclaimed.

"Then you'd better get moving so I don't have to."

Irsu rushed to his water basin and grabbed a towel. It smelled like one would expect a towel to smell if that towel had been used for a month with no visit to the washboard. He soaked his face and then wiped with it anyway. He brushed his hair, then grabbed a few beads to weave into his beard during the walk to the throne room.

"Now, Sir Crackstone."

"Sir?" he asked. "I'm no blooded warrior."

"Not yet," she said cryptically, "but most of our boys eventually are, even secondborns like you. Forgive me for jumping the gun and trying to be nice to you." She pointed toward the doorway, since he'd not built a door yet. "Let's go."

Not him. He wasn't made for war. He was going to set up his hearth and build the population of Iron Mountain if he had any say at all on the matter.

Strolling out into the hall with her, he was aware that the daily masses could come and go from his open home as they wished. Hopefully nobody would think his hammers and chisels would look better at their hearth than his.

"What's your name?" he asked the messenger. "I've never met you before."

"I imagine with the work we do our paths don't cross much," she responded. "I'm Kordina. Kordina Bloodstone."

He stopped, and two steps later she turned to look at him. Then rolled her eyes.

"No, I'm not a princess, I'm a cousin. You haven't been relaxed in any formalities. Let's go."

He fell back into stride beside her, wondering what the official titles were for a royal cousin. Her semi-glossiness? Her mostly polishedness?

"What are you thinking about, looking at me like that?" she asked, accusation in her voice. "This is why I hate telling anyone my last name."

"I get it," he replied. "I was just wondering if you had an honorary I should be using."

"I have no honors to my name. Or to me. I deliver messages and take notes."

"Someone's got to do it," he said, realizing he'd hit a sore spot. "You seem to do it well, and that carries honor."

She shook her head, but she was smiling. "You're a funny one, Irsu Crackstone. Here we are, at the audience hall. You'll follow me inside. Once the steward recognizes me, I'll present you."

"Fair enough."

They walked through large gold doors into the hall, only to be stopped a few steps beyond the threshold by guards. "Wait," they intoned simultaneously.

Several minutes passed as Irsu and Kordina did exactly that. Curtains blocked the view of the audience hall, Irsu had no idea what was going on past the small area he was in. He made small talk with the messenger.

"Miss Kordina Bloodstone, royal courier, cousin to the Underking," someone said from deeper in the room.

"That's us. Wait for me to call your name," she told him as she stepped through the curtains.

Another few minutes passed, he shuffled his feet as the guards stared past him like he didn't exist. He figured if he did anything wrong they'd notice him. But then he wouldn't exist for long.

Kordina was speaking on the other side of the curtain.

"Noble Underking, I present Irsu Crackstone, second son of his line, son of Morat Crackstone, deceased, and Dame Syledna Crackstone, living in honor as the bearer of two warriors. Here be Irsu Crackstone, your summoned subject."

Irsu stepped through the curtain.

The hall was smaller than he expected, maybe twenty persons were present. The Underking sat on a stone throne, which dominated the far end of the room. Most of the decorating budget must have been spent on the outer doors, the walls in here were mushwood and creepwood, not the gold inlaid granite he'd expected. A few people stood beside the king on the dais, more lined the walls on both sides as he entered the room, sitting on stone bleachers carved from the heartrock of Iron Mountain.

The King stood up. "Irsu, come forward. I haven't seen you in years, since the sendoff for your father to the great beyond."

Irsu stepped forward as commanded. He'd been so young when his father died defending the mountain that he had no memory of the man or of the King attending his funeral. Mother had never mentioned it.

"I have a task for you, a strange one for a secondborn," the king said, "but a great honor. It's a chance to represent the Iron Mountains and secure a future for your people.

What? That sounded like it wasn't about him building a hearth… or finishing up the one he was working on anyway. "Anything, my king," Irsu responded, kneeling.

"Oh, get up. I want you to go fight in the joining of worlds, not learn all this pageantry and show."

Irsu stood up, confused. To be honest, he always felt that's what royalty was about. Pageantry and show. Also, as he'd told Kordina, he was no warrior. And he had no idea what a joining of the worlds was.

"Irsu," King Bloodstone said, sweeping his arm, "I can see you're confused. I'd like to fix that. This is Veinstriker Veznik. Priest of Ekesstu. He's had a vision he's going to share with you."

Irsu looked at the priest. He'd never been one for going to temple. It seemed to him that prosperity was more about swinging a pick at the right rock or making excellence with one's work than it was about the plans of any deities.

"Citizen Crackstone, I can sense your skepticism. In fact, I think if not for the fact that the Underking summoned you, you'd not even be here."

"I'd be finishing up the coal bin in my hearth," Irsu said, smirking. "Why would I be here without a summons?"

Veznik blushed. "I mean you wouldn't have come to hear the words of a priest."

Irsu shrugged after looking at the king. No sense lying about it. "I'm not particularly aware of the gods having much influence in my life."

In many places those words would earn him a flogging, or a crucifixion, or a banishment. But in Iron Mountain clan, truth was revered as the path to follow. For that reason, despite the gasps in the court observers sitting on benches lining the walls, he felt safe enough speaking his mind.

"Yes, I sense that," the priest continued. "You're a soul who walks his own path, but then wonders why he never meets anyone on it."

A few snickering voices erupted in the hall. Irsu had to be fair and admit the priest had stung him back. He liked Veznik better for it.

The King's stern visage silenced them.

"I apologize," Veznik said. "That wasn't phrased well, and was uncalled for." He pulled a glass vial on a leather strap from his pocket. "To the business you've been called here for. This is sacred soil, from my temple. It originally came from a place called the *Lost Hold*." He put the soil away. "Have you heard of it?"

"I haven't."

"Are you a fan of history? Do you avoid reading your scrolls, as your brother said?"

"Bordnu spends too much time in his. He doesn't live life, he reads it," Irsu answered in irritation. How dare his brother speak ill of him outside the family?

The King was clearly growing tired of the verbal prancing. He waved Veznik into silence. "The Lost Hold is a place our people built ten thousand years ago. In that age we were legion in number, and we could do anything. We built an entire hold without anyone else knowing."

"Where is this hold?" Irsu asked. How does one hide a construction project on that scale?

"On Earth. And we're going back to reclaim it," King Bloodstone replied.

"With all due respect, my king, Earth must be far away. I've never heard of it."

"It's a place you will know well soon enough," the King told him.

Irsu didn't know what to say. He didn't want to travel.

"I've selected five of our greatest warriors for the trip, one to lead Iron Company, four to lead the platoons of Iron Company. But the priest said I had to include you, so I've sacked one of those great warriors and instead you're going to train to lead one of the platoons."

Irsu wasn't a fighter. He'd never held a weapon in anger in his life. "W-w-what?"

"Stand up!" the king bellowed. "You're a warrior now. Act like one."

Irsu straightened himself.

"For the next four years, you will train with Hearthstone Platoon. You will learn the axe. You will learn the pike. You will learn the dagger and the crossbow. You will get to know the soldiers under your command. You will get to know your second. And you will get to know yourself."

"I'm—"

"No warrior?" the priest interrupted. "You might as well claim you're not a dwarf. I have seen you leading the way into the Lost Hold. I have the vision."

"The vision?" Irsu questioned.

"I see things," Veznik answered. "Things that come true."

The world swirled around him. He only wanted to finish his hearth, find a good female to marry, settle down and carry on the family name like any good second son. It was Bordnu's job to fight for the clan.

The Underking looked horrified. "Is he going to pa—"

The world went black.

Chapter 2 - Makalu

October 8, 1938

Oberstleutnant Ernst Haufmann pulled his parka tighter around himself. Fifty-eight hundred meters up the face of a wretched mountain in the northeastern edge of Nepal, he was cold and just continuing to breathe was the biggest chore he'd ever had.

Wind blew past, carrying snow directly sideways and trying to hurl him onto the rock spires below. Snow shouldn't move horizontally. It should drop peacefully from the sky to settle on Bavarian pines.

Someone grabbed his arm.

It was that skinny self-righteous bastard Gustaf Meckler. Religious idiot. Ernst considered, for a moment, throwing Meckler off the side of the mountain. In the end, it was his own exhaustion that saved Meckler's life. Plus he wasn't sure he could take down the Heereshilfpfarrer in his current state.

"Oberstleutnant," Meckler yelled after lowering his mask. "We are almost there. Concentrate on the mission."

"Yah," Ernst sighed. Even talking drained him. "You are in good shape for a Chaplain."

Meckler grinned.

For the next quarter mile Ernst concentrated on the ice covered rock trail cut into the mountain face. No more than a meter wide at any point, leaving the trail would almost certainly be instant death. The edge wasn't exactly a precipice, but the slope was enough that anyone going over would keep falling for a kilometer or more.

"There!" Meckler yelled.

An audible gasp of relief collectively escaped the lips of the two dozen Gebirgsjäger troops slogging along behind him. Not normally one to feel sympathy for another, Ernst actually savored his twinge of sympathy for his men. To Ernst, it was proof of his humanity. Despite the fact that they each carried a twenty kilo load of supplies and weapons, while Ernst carried nothing but his parka, his binoculars, and his Luger pistol.

Meckler raced ahead, although how he did it was beyond comprehension. Even the native guides weren't spending energy so stupidly.

A semi-circle of buildings somehow adhered to a cliff face, seeming to defy gravity as they jutted out over the precipice. The trail continued past the buildings, but to take it one had to go through the midst of the buildings themselves. By all but the most recent standards, this was an unassailable fort.

Fortunately times change, and Ernst had machine guns and explosives to assist him should they be needed.

As the German party approached the gate that barred the path, a monk in bright orange robes stood on the other side. Resting his hand on the grip of his pistol, Ernst walked up to the iron bars of the gate. From the looks of it, the barrier only opened from the inside.

"Ask him if we can come in," Ernst ordered his native translator.

Before the translator could speak, the monk responded in German as perfect as if he were a Berlin native.

"Oberstleutnant, Cloud Master Lahkpa is eager to meet you," the man said. "Of course you may come in."

Ernst pushed his scarf back up over the skin of his face, wondering how it could be the monk wasn't a frozen corpse. As he did so, the monk cranked away on a lever that winched up the gate into the stone wall above it.

Meckler nearly knocked a Sherpa over the edge as he rushed past to go inside.

Idiot.

"Inside, men," Ernst ordered and gestured his men past him. "Ready your MP-40s, just in case," he told two of them as they passed. Both did as commanded.

If it was a trap, let Meckler pay the price for his eagerness. And the guns were now between any potential enemy and Ernst, as they should be.

"That is not necessary," the monk said. "We have been expecting you, and you are welcome here. Come inside, and let the warmth of the Mother warm you. We have food, drink, and places to rest."

"Your hospitality is most kind," Ernst replied. "But we must be sure."

"Of course."

Once everyone was inside, Ernst followed. The monastery looked like even more of a fort inside the small courtyard. The buildings were impressive, but the structure also extended back into the mountainside.

"In the womb of the Mother is the key you have come for," the monk informed Ernst. "Follow me."

Despite the blowing snow, the orange robe was easy to follow. Iron bound wooden doors sealed the mountain from the outside, and Ernst was shocked to see two swastikas centered on each door. Each made of iron, and each a half meter across.

Meckler practically danced with anticipation. "Do you see?" the idiot asked, pointing at the swastikas. "We are here as part of a bigger plan."

"You two," Ernst said to the machine gunners. "Take the front. Do not fire your weapons unless we are threatened."

"Is that really necessary?" Meckler asked. "They clearly welcome our arrival."

"Heereshilfpfarrer Meckler, I have hardly the breath to stand, let alone answer your stupid questions. Do not vex me."

The fool shut his face, and if Ernst cared about religion or believed in a deity, he'd call that a blessing.

The doors opened, and a long hallway disappeared into the distance. It was dimly lit every hundred meters or so by torches guttering in their sconces.

"Behind me," Ernst ordered Meckler just to annoy the man.

Following the monk and his two soldiers, the rest of the team walked into the corridor. The unending rock stretched for a kilometer into the mountainside. Every centimeter was carved with symbology, and many times water from the Earth itself ran into the corridor on one side, and out of the other side through channels the water had cut into the rock. This tunnel was old, at least a few centuries if not more. It was all the more remarkable that Ernst saw the occasional swastika carved into the stone. If this was real, someone long dead saw the Germans coming. The carvings ended about twenty meters before the tunnel opened up into a natural cavern.

An old woman in dark brown robes stood at the start of a path into the cavern. The cave was large, something Ernst knew only because of the reflections glinting off stone in the distance. The only light was coming from a host of torches arrayed around a pillar. Outside the circle of torches half a dozen buildings stood, possibly living spaces for the guardians of whatever the monks kept here.

"I am Lahkpa," the old woman said, also in perfect German.

"I am Oberstleutnant Ernst Haufmann," he replied. "How is it you speak my tongue?"

"We have seen your coming," she replied. "There is no reason to delay. You came for a key, and a key you will have."

The cooperative attitude of the monks was a relief. While he had no qualms about using force to secure relics for the Reich, he liked it best when those relics were simply handed over. In this case, whatever made these people realize the Germans would come for their key was a gift that avoided bloodshed.

"You already have the Intepna Hojarr?" Lahkpa asked.

Ernst almost stopped walking, the question shocked him so much. That was another relic that he'd simply walked in and taken. In northern Finland. A small stone church built for pagan religions ages ago had housed the Intepna, and the Samu herders who guarded it had simply waved the Germans in and walked off. Not a word was exchanged as Ernst's team walked away with the prize.

"How did you know of that?" he asked the woman.

"Eyes are not just for seeing what is here," she answered. "They are also for seeing what is there."

What did that mean? Cryptic nonsense.

"As you say," Ernst replied, not wishing to discourage her cooperative stance.

She gestured toward the only lit area in the cave. "The Inshu Key is housed in the pillar we are walking to. Once we get there, you may simply take it if you like. I would appreciate if you allowed us to bless it one more time before you go, however."

"I could use the rest, as could my men," Ernst said. "We have come a long way in terrain we are not used to traveling."

"I know," she said. "But you must take the key and go after the blessing. The sooner you get it to the Intepna Hojarr, the better."

"Why is that?" he asked.

"Because the prophecies say so," she replied. "It is how it is supposed to be done."

He smiled to mask his irritation.

"Here we are," she said as they entered the flickering circle of light.

A dozen monks walked from the buildings, momentarily alarming his two men on guard. The monks carried long curved blades, thin, tarnished with age, and clearly meant to kill if turned to such ends.

The guards raised their submachine guns, ready to fire on Ernst's command.

"Hold," Ernst ordered. "There will be a ritual. I think their weapons are part of that."

Two dozen Germans, a dozen Sherpas and a baker's dozen of the monks gathered within the circle of torches surrounding the pillar. Ernst followed Lahkpa around to the far side of the ten meter high obelisk.

A small cubby contained a felt pillow. On it was a disk with a diamond shaped projection on one side. Two candles burned next to the pillow.

As Ernst stared inside the receptacle at his prize, the monks began to chant. The other Germans, less on edge since the monks didn't seem hostile, took off their packs, sat down and waited.

Above the cubby two overlapping circles began to glow a dim blue, and a similar shape glowed on the disk key itself. Ernst laughed inside at the petty magician tricks the monks used to bolster their own faith.

The chanting raised in tone, and the Sherpas that guided the Germans up the mountain suddenly cried out in alarm. They grabbed their satchels and prepared to leave.

The two machine gunners stood, prepared to answer any order that Ernst might give.

"They can't leave, how will we get down the mountain!" Meckler barked.

That sealed Ernst's decision. "Let them go, if they are cowards," he ordered. "There are no branches on the trail down the mountain. We will secure new guides in the valley."

Meckler looked properly annoyed, which pleased Ernst.

Ten minutes later the Sherpas were all gone.

"What alarmed them?" Ernst asked Lahkpa.

"Lack of religious vision," the old woman answered. "And now I give you the key."

She reached into the cubby, picked up the mushroom shaped artifact, and turned toward Ernst. "Do not be alarmed by my fate."

Two monks moved in behind her as she dropped the item into Ernst's hand. They rapidly pulled knives from their robes and then drove the blades into the back of the old woman.

Lahkpa smiled as blood poured from her mouth before dropping to her knees then collapsing.

Ernst stared at the two monks ahead of him, stunned as they raised their knives once again. The other monks in the circle did the same. He started to give the order to gun them down, but it was too late for that. The monks did the job for him. They each turned their knives point up and drove the tip into their heads from under the jaw.

Thirteen orange robed figures dropped to the ground, dead.

The blue circles on the pillar and the key flared brightly for a moment, then winked out. Only the torchlight remained.

Ernst laughed as he tucked the Inshu Key into a small wooden box he'd brought to contain it.

"Pick up your things," he ordered. "We have a long trip home."

Chapter 3 - The Truce of Hagirr

Irsu stood near the front of his platoon.

The gate was about a ten minute march away, or at least would be if the way was clear. A horde of soldiers stretched between him and the lost world. Everyone nearby was restless, but this was the day foretold in the Eradna-Hagirr. A day that could not be rushed. The day of Bonding, when Aerth and Earth once more become as one world.

A dragon circled overhead, a black with beautiful outstretched wings catching thermals from the valley floor. Normally Irsu would set his dwarves ready to receive the fury of such a beast, but today, as for the last year or so, an uncomfortable truce existed.

More dragons floated in the eastern sky, morning sun glinted off their metallic scales. Lower, elven air raiders circled their griffins and pegasi around gnomish airships.

"If not for the Truce of Hagirr, today would be the bloodiest day Aerth has ever seen," Irsu's assistant platoon leader, Coragg said.

"A sharp axe will be a necessity in the coming days regardless of what we see now," Irsu assured him. "Once we cross over, I'd bet my beard the truce will not hold. My beard isn't bold enough. By the Underking's beard, I swear it." He gestured toward the elven warriors halfway between them and the gate. "You don't get a lasting peace with the likes of that around."

"I'm surprised it's held this long with so many enemies in such proximity," a voice said behind him.

Before he even turned toward the voice, Irsu's face unleashed a rare smile. "Bordnu," he said, grinning even more widely as he turned to face his brother. He waved a hand toward Bordnu's shoulder insignia. Captain of the Iron. "You mean they are still going to let you lead this company?"

"The king knows talent when he sees it," Bordnu replied, his own grin as wide as an axe head.

The two brothers locked arms and slammed their foreheads together despite the fine helms they wore.

"I have hope of living through this thing we are doing then, thanks to the king's wisdom," Irsu said. "Do you know when we march?"

"The gate has opened. The dragons have sent through their scout. He has not returned," Bordnu answered. "When he does, Hagirr will tell us the plan."

"That wizard!" Irsu complained. "How is it our forefathers bound our service today to a human? And a magician at that."

"Do you not read the scrolls still?" Bordnu asked, laughing. "That is why I am commander of this company, and you are leader of this platoon, Irsu. Education."

"Aye, but I'm prettier," Irsu countered.

"Ma always thought so," his brother agreed. "Explains why you didn't study your scrolls, and were always sneaking off to mingle beards with the ladies."

Irsu shrugged. Beer, fighting, ladies, and his newly built hearth in Iron Mountain. What else was there? Leading the other dwarves in battle put their fates on his shoulders, something he'd only reluctantly agreed to accept when asked. Asked was a friendly term for what happened, of course, as he wasn't really given a choice. What the Underking asks is a directive, not a request.

"There is movement at the gate," Coragg said. "The dragon returns."

Irsu and Bordnu turned to face the news.

A flash of light signaled the arrival of the wizard, Hagirr. It was he, ten thousand years earlier who had discovered Earth. Then he'd broken the two worlds he'd joined for long enough to achieve his goals apart. And the reason no humans other than Hagirr walked Aerth today. He'd sent them to the other world, knowing that failure to separate the humans from the other races of the world would result in a war of extinction.

And the humans would have lost.

For the same reasons any of the other races that entered Earth had sworn to leave once it was ready for the humans. And magic enforced their word.

It was Hagirr that had foreseen the worlds being rejoined, hoping that on Earth his own kind would prosper and grow strong enough to survive in the ten thousand years since. Had they? Or was humanity dead? Irsu had no idea. The dragon would tell everyone soon enough.

By agreement, Earth would now belong to all. The humans had their time. That was the deal. Time to get strong, then they would be tested.

Someone had activated the gate from the far side, just as foretold.

Something had set the trial of humanity in motion.

Irsu's axe physically vibrated in his hand, so thunderous was the noise around him.

How Hagirr had lived to see the rejoining, Irsu didn't know. He knew little of humanity, except legends and tales mothers told to scare children to sleep. However the wizard lived, it was probably rooted in evil. That's why the dwarves and elves had gone to war with humanity in the first place.

The evil in the hearts of Men.

Bordnu would argue that there was no proof black magic was involved in Hagirr's longevity. Irsu didn't need proof. Because for one to prosper so, another must be deprived. This was true in wealth and life. Balance was the nature of things. It was why Irsu tried hard not to take more than he needed for a good life.

The dragon exited the gate well off the ground, then hovered over the legions at the front of the horde.

"I am Rodimikari! I have seen Earth!" the dragon's voice bellowed across the valley.

A million voices went silent at once. The assemblage was so quiet, Irsu heard the breeze whistling through the helmet visors of his unit.

Emptiness made his ears ring.

The wizard gestured. The dragon responded, and while Irsu could not hear the human, he heard the response.

"There is war among the sons of Earth. Humans are everywhere, and they've created devices for traveling the ground and air almost gnomish in their design. Magic is still faded from that world, but as Hagirr said it would, it is flowing in through the gate, and will soon be reborn. The humans attacked me as one would expect. There were rightfully afraid."

Silence as the wizard gestured some more.

"War has leveled the city that houses the gates. There was no sign of the old gods, only a new god that did not answer the pleas of the humans I burned away."

Gesturing from Hagirr, probably angry words as well if Irsu had to guess.

"They attacked me, I merely defended myself. Who has the gall to attack Rodimikari? While magic is all but gone from Earth, their weapons have grown powerful. I felt the sting of a thousand tiny arrows."

A moment as the conversation continued from the wizard.

"We can advance. The lands of Earth will see the children of Aerth. Send in your elves, wizard. Your gnomes. Your dwarves. Your goblins, trolls, and whatever has climbed up from the slime of the lands to serve you. I, Rodimikari, will lead my people back to

Earth, to once more claim the skies as we did in the days of my fathers."

That's right. Irsu remembered now. Dragons had come here from Earth. And humans had gone there. A trade the dragons had readily agreed to in order to once again wield the magic that was dying on their home world.

When the first gate was open those thousands of years ago, the Dwarves had spent time on Earth as well. Mining wealth, building holds, and preparing the places that would hold the keys to reopen the gate today.

Obviously those long dead dwarves had done their jobs well, as the gate was activated, standing before him, ready to receive those who would go through.

"Irsu," Bordnu said, pointing toward the platoon. "It is our last time to prepare. Have your dwarves polish their armor and sharpen their axes. In the morning we will likely move forward."

"Aye," Irsu agreed.

The dragon flew off toward the mountains, and Irsu waited, almost holding his breath as the next moments of silence lay unbroken.

Then the noise started anew, and his axes sang in his hands once more from the cacophony.

Movement began at the front of the assembly, near the Hagirr gate. Almost a mile wide and a quarter of that tall, the gate was the only passage to the new world. Four giants stood and walked through it, followed by a contingent of dwarves from another mountain chain in a land far from here.

"It has begun," Bordnu said.

"It will be a few days before we can pass," Irsu responded. "But when we do, you know the plan?"

"I have been briefed by the King directly," his brother answered. "We will march on our ancient homes, and once more take what was always ours."

"That is not how Hagirr will see it."

"We built the holds. We mined. We prepared. It is the dwarves who deserved that world. Not humans, insane that they are."

"And if the humans the dragon spoke of are not agreeable to that?"

Bordnu shrugged. "Then they die."

"Hagirr will not set easy with that solution," Irsu said.

"The Underking believes that the magic that keeps the wizard alive will not work on Earth. That if the wizard crosses over, he will turn to dust."

"Do you believe the same?"

"Why else would he not have gone with his people those many years ago?"

"Good. Then we will make Earth ours."

"For the Underking."

"For our people," Irsu countered. "Dwarves don't need magic. Earth is perfect for us."

"For our people," Bordnu agreed.

Chapter 4 - Running

May 19, 1940

Sergeant Harold Hughes smoked with his mate, Corporal Timothy Martin. The two men comprised the light machine gun crew for their squad in the 5th Infantry Division, 25th Infantry Brigade.

They were attached to a Matador lorry, part of a planned counterattack against the German forces sweeping through northern France. Intended solely to buy time for the evacuation of British Expeditionary Forces, the attack was a death warrant for the men involved. It was unlikely there would be time to extract the infantry sections on the line, and even if there were time, losses would be staggering under the attentions of the Luftwaffe and the German mobile units.

Scuttlebutt was that De Gaulle was moving French forces north to the south of Lille, which might take some of Hitler's heat off Harry and Tim's unit, but rumors were running wild.

"When we get out of this, Timothy, I think I'll have a steak."

"A steak Harry? A night with the missus?"

"What has she done to deserve a steak?" Harry asked.

Both men laughed. They knew they weren't getting out of this.

"You pick up extra ammo?" Tim asked.

"Twelve magazines off lads headed out. What's that?" Harry chewed his lips as he tried to do math.

"About a minute of fire plus the time to change the magazines," Tim told him.

"You're slow as hell at that, so probably five minutes then."

"That's bollocks, that's what that is," Tim protested. "You're lucky to have me."

"That I am, mate. I got us some extra smokes."

"Good man."

Their conversation was interrupted by the drone of fighters overhead. The two men set up their gun as best they could, but the enemy wasn't attacking them. Stukas were flying over, headed west, toward richer target areas. Rumors that the Luftwaffe were strafing the roads with civilian traffic were unconfirmed, but Harry knew why they'd do it. The British Expeditionary Forces couldn't retreat if the roads weren't open. And Hitler would love nothing more than to capture or kill the entirety of British forces on the continent.

A lieutenant ran up to their lorry, out of breath.

"Sir?" Harry said. Everyone was too tired, too stressed to salute. Such normalcy could come later.

"You're moving out, Sergeant. Load up your men, see that vehicle over there? Follow it. Your driver has been briefed. You'll be setting up east of Arras to slow the Krauts down."

"Right away, Lieutenant," Harry answered.

The young man extended his hand. "Godspeed, Sergeant."

Harry knew what that meant. While he and his men headed to Arras, the lieutenant would be headed to Dunkirk for evacuation. "And to you, sir."

He watched the young officer run off to the next vehicle, then shook his head.

Picking up his machine gun, he slapped Tim on the back and yelled at the other men around him. "You heard him, boys. In the back. We're off. We've been wished Godspeed, so I'm sure we're in for a leisurely stroll by the river with tea after."

The men laughed as they loaded up. At least they were in good spirits. Sometimes that happened to men who knew they'd die for a cause.

As they got in line and drove away to their fate, Harry sat in the back and looked out of the canvas at the French countryside. They passed a French family going the other way, headed toward the coast. Two young ladies, smiling despite being mud covered and haggardly tired, waved at the British soldiers. It was as if they knew the men were going to hold off the enemy coming for them and wanted to say their thanks.

"Not many young men among them," Tim noticed from across the lorry's bed.

"I didn't see a one," Harry agreed. "Another generation sent into the mud, lives forfeit to men who don't get their hands dirty."

"Pitiful," one of the men from the front of the bench said. "We should drag that lot out here with us."

"The men who send us to war have no conscience," Harry added. "And when war comes, it wounds us all, except those old men who start it."

Chapter 5 - Rotterdam

May 20, 1940

Ernst's driver stopped his car near downtown. Rotterdam was heavily bombed, the Luftwaffe had done a job on it. A few buildings still burned nearby, but most were simply rubble. A church stood, one of the few structures still intact.

The Saint Lawrence Cathedral showed a few scars, but it would do for Ernst's purposes.

"Bring the things," he ordered Meckler.

As he climbed the steps to the sanctuary, he heard Meckler bellowing orders behind him. The same two dozen soldiers he'd commanded for the last five years snapped to their duties.

Within the hour the situation was arranged. The Intepna Hojarr sat on the altar of the church. The Inshu Key was in Ernst's hands. Meckler stood beside him, practically tittering with excitement.

"Here, Meckler. You may do the honors," Ernst said. "We have worked a long time for this."

Meckler's face displayed how unexpected Ernst's kind act was. It was a slight surprise to Ernst as well, but he had an uneasy feeling about the ritual that was soon to unfold. Even if that ritual was just inserting and turning the key.

"Herr Hitler has given approval?"

"Yah," Ernst said. "I spoke to him myself. You may begin."

Meckler took the Inshu Key, then walked up to the altar. He crossed himself in front of the crucifix on the back wall. The Intepna Hojarr was a hammered iron box, approximately a meter long, about half that wide and tall. A depression rested on the top, a gear that connected to other gears under the lid. Two overlapping circles etched into the top of the box matched those on the top of the key. The same ones on the monolith Ernst had found it in.

Of course Meckler gave a speech. Irritating fool.

"Today, we finally tap into the power of other worlds," the chaplain said. "We finally harvest the power of the mystical world for the Führer, for the Fatherland. Today, with the insertion and turning of this key, we seal the fate of our enemies."

Meckler placed the stone key into the geared slot. For the first time that Ernst had seen, the gear on the box turned. A seam opened around the top of the Intepna Hojarr, one he'd not seen before. Blue light flared on the key and the box, emanating from the overlapping circles.

The lid popped open and two orbs jumped into the air over the altar. They glowed dimly with the same blue light the circles shone with, and grew brighter as Ernst watched.

The orbs began to rotate about each other, and then grew closer together. A whooshing sound grew in volume as the orbs cut through the air. After a few minutes, as the Germans watched in stunned silence, the orbs touched and overlapped, just as the circle symbology on the key and case did.

That was when the world changed. A circular field popped into being and began expanding. The church crumbled around him, and a mixture of dry earth and dead grass appeared where the church floor was a moment before. Ernst heard Meckler scream something, but he could no longer see Meckler.

The altar area was gone.

Ernst and his men broke for the door of the church. He had no idea what he was seeing, but the primal screams still coming from an unseen Meckler more than broke his will to remain. Ernst's driver headed toward the car, but Ernst pushed him out of the way. "Get in the other side," the Oberstleutnant yelled.

As he jumped into the drivers seat the sphere emanating from the Intepna Hojarr burst through the walls of the church, and as it did they collapsed. Some of the debris hit the ground, the rest of it and the roof of the church disappeared into the orb.

He slammed the car into reverse, once up to speed turned the wheels sharply and the vehicle spun around to face the other way. He popped it into gear and mashed the accelerator to the floor.

The sphere seemed to be expanding at a few meters per second now. As he looked in the rear view mirror the church was gone. A hemispherical bubble was approaching the waters of the docks already.

Then something he'd never erase from his mind crossed the barrier. A winged creature, looking much like the dragons of European lore, stepped into Ernst's world. German soldiers occupying the city center opened fire on it.

Then it opened fire on them.

Flames erupted from its mouth, bathing the ground in liquid hot death.

Ernst almost wrecked he was so engrossed in the events he saw in the mirror. Only the screams of the driver saved them, and the car swerved around bombing rubble at the last second.

"*Wir haben das Tor zur Hölle geöffnet*," the driver screamed again.

Yes, Ernst agreed in his mind. We have opened the gates of Hell.

It remained to be seen if that was a smart thing or something else entirely.

Chapter 6 - Hell's Spawn

May 22, 1940

"Harry, we have new orders," Timothy told him. "We're to head North to rendezvous with a Belgian contingent holding a line near Roeselare."

Six Spitfires roared overhead, no more than five hundred feet above the ground.

"What's the point?" Harry asked. "We've only now made it to Arras. We can die here as easily as there."

"Rumor has it something's happened to draw the Germans from the front," Timothy answered. "We're to take advantage of it."

"Where'd you hear this?"

"Radioman. That Miller fellow. He told me when he was heating up some bread on the lorry's manifold."

"We taking the Matador? Or do we have to walk to our end?"

"They're making the French civilians that were going to take our lorry walk to Dunkirk, not that it will do them any good. We're to keep it and put it to good use, according to the brass. We've an hour to make the line."

"Seems like the officers would have come to tell us."

"Not many of those still here," Timothy observed. "We uneducated men hold the reigns now."

"Right. Then let's get to it." Harry ordered. "We can complain about our lot on the way."

It took five minutes to load the men and their equipment into the lorry. Five minutes after that they were pushing thirty miles per hour toward Roeselare. The road wasn't great, the ride was rough, but in Harry's mind that was proof he still had life in his body.

"I think I'll buy the missus that steak after all," he informed Timothy.

"Of course you will," Timothy said, patronization all over his face. Corporal Martin fully expected this to be his last day.

"No, you misunderstand me," Harry said. "This was all a grand adventure until the last few days. I've come to realize I'd like nothing more than to watch her smile as she enjoys a meal. I'd spend my days with her, feeding the chickens, seeing to the farm. And spoil her until she's fat."

Timothy shook a pack of smokes Harry'd given him earlier and handed one over. He looked Harry in the eye. "You weren't listening, mate. I said of course you will. You'll be shaggin' 'er right in a few weeks."

"That's not a proper way to talk about a man's woman," Harry said, unsure how offended he should be.

"Does this seem like a time to be proper?" Tim asked him.

It wasn't. It was a time to say it out, in as few words as possible because words took time.

"You going to get hooked up with your girl?" Harry asked.

"She quit me two months ago," Timothy replied. "I got it in the post last week."

Harry looked down at the unlit cigarette in his fingers. "Stupid, how the world does a man."

Tim lit his cigarette, then leaned over and lit Harry's. "What' the saying Harry? Plenty of fish?"

"Lot's of 'em," he agreed.

They rode together in silence for a bit, letting the words between them rest silent.

It was all too soon the lorry ground one of its gears as they pulled to a stop. Harry jumped out onto the grass, then looked north toward where the Germans would attack from.

He didn't expect to see what he saw there, but the driver had stopped short of their destination and Harry knew why.

A hole appeared to cover much of the northern sky, almost as if someone had set a bowl upside down on the ground. A bowl that had to be dozens of miles across.

"What in the name of Pete is that?" Tim asked, standing next to him.

A few miles north three German aircraft crossed from east to west, two Bf-109s and a Stuka trailing behind. The fighters had abandoned the dive bomber to a fate Harry hadn't dreamed of in his worst nightmares, let alone expected to see.

A black winged beast, several times the size of the German dive bomber, pounced on it from behind. As fast as the aircraft was, the creature was faster, and significantly so. It shredded the Stuka, and pieces rained from the sky. Moments later, now hovering in the air, the creature made motions that could only have one conclusion.

It had eaten the pilot.

"Like a bloody oyster," Timothy said.

"If you wouldn't mind, wake me up," Harry replied, stunned.

"We must both be asleep and dreaming," Timothy assured him.

The six Spitfires they'd seen earlier raced upward from near the ground, spilling machine gun fire into the beast. The impacts sparked against it, almost as if the fighters were attacking the thickest armor plate.

The creature roared, something they heard even at this distance.

A more distant roar answered from further north, and Harry was suddenly very sad for the lads flying those planes.

Fire erupted from the black monster and one of the Spitfires exploded in a ball of debris and smoke. Seconds later a second followed as a second creature responded to the call from the first.

Being sensible, the Spitfires turned and ran south, almost directly toward the Matador and Harry's squad. His men were gathered in a semicircle around the front of the vehicle, watching the aerial battle.

"Get to cover," Harry yelled at them.

A small stone wall was all they had.

Accepting of any shelter facing the unknown enemy, the men huddled on the ground as the first Spitfire flew over a few hundred yards east of them and maybe fifty yards off the ground. A second soon followed, immediately trailed by one of the creatures.

It was massive and green, and the wings that swept from its body pushed a torrent of air down over the men. Dust rose in great blasts, forcing them to close their eyes and shelter their faces.

A grinding sound and an explosion shortly thereafter let them know one of the Spitfires was gone. The roaring sound of a propeller faded with distance, as did the pulse of the creature's wing beats.

Harry dared a view over the top of the stone wall, and was immediately shocked by what greeted him.

A German soldier stood there, his hands up, his K98 rifle and a pistol on the ground next to him.

Jumping up from his shelter, Harry pulled his own pistol on the man.

"I surrender," the German yelled in English. "We are not enemies! Not anymore."

Harry leaned over and grabbed the man, then yanked him over the fence. He forced the German to the ground with his back on the grass, then sat on top of him.

Harry realized then how vulnerable they'd been. The German's rifle was on the ground, at the spot he surrendered. The Kraut could easily have killed some of the British squad had he wanted.

That didn't keep Harry from holding his pistol to the man's head.

Seconds later another Spitfire raced overhead, with a black beast on its tail. That one, Harry knew, liked to eat pilots. He said a quick prayer for the aviator, then turned his attention back to the German.

"You speak American English?"

"I lived in America for several years," the man said. Harry was surprised there wasn't fear in the Hun's voice. His uniform was showered in blood splatters, and traces of blood lined the man's face.

"What happened to you? Is that your blood?"

The prisoner glanced down at his uniform. "No. Not mine."

"What happened?" Harry repeated.

"Can you not see?" The German pointed south. "Something has changed, we are all in the grips of death now."

"What were those things? A German weapon?"

"Gott, no!" the man replied, laughing. "At first we thought they were British weapons. Then we saw the Spitfires, and your men started dying with ours."

"That doesn't explain this blood," Timothy demanded. "Explain that."

"Those are not the only beasts coming through," the German replied.

"Through what?"

"Can you not see? That thing, in the north. It is over Rotterdam, it is where the creatures are coming from. Rotterdam is gone."

"Gone? What do you mean gone?"

"I mean what I just said. The city isn't there anymore, it is some other place now, or just gone. A world connected to ours, maybe? Hell, maybe? *Ich vice nicht.*"

"That's the thing in the sky," Timothy said. "Judgment day."

"Yah," the German agreed.

"Bullshite," Harry said. "Those were dragons, I know the legends. God's angels don't look like dragons."

The man under him shrugged. "It is bad, whatever. There is more than dragons."

"Like what?" Harry pressed.

"Faeries. Giants. Armored creatures with axes. More I do not know."

One of Harry's men tapped on his back. "Sergeant, you best look at this."

"Stay down," Harry told the German as he got up and moved to the stone wall to look.

The wall they were behind was near the top of a hundred foot hill. The ground sloped downward to the north, into a line of trees.

Something was emerging from the trees.

Stout men, in iron armor, like the knights of old. The armor was black, and each carried either a two headed axe or…

"Are those crossbows?" Timothy asked.

Harry looked to his right, surprised to find the German between him and Tim, looking at the new arrivals as well. No matter. The German just became important to taking one step toward equalizing their number against a potential enemy. "What's your name?"

"Hans."

"Hans, you're going to need your gun. I'm not getting it."

Hans looked at him uncertainly for a moment, then nodded. He jumped over the fence, grabbed his weapon, then jumped back as two bolts whizzed past him.

That made it clear the armored fellows were hostile. Harry's risk of Han's life had netted him two benefits. One more gun and clarity.

"They must have tracked you," Harry said. "You led them to us."

"Those men, or others like them, butchered my unit," Hans said. "Thirty-nine well trained soldiers killed, unless some survived like me."

"How did you get away?" Timothy asked him.

"I ran."

Harry sighed, but it was hard to condemn Hans. It was one thing to fight men, but dragons and whatever these were? Harry might have ran on first contact too. But he was wasn't surprised, and while this was first contact, it wasn't completely uninformed. Not this time. He peeked over the fence down the hill. A hundred of the short fellows gathered at the bottom, forming into a line.

"Line warfare?" Timothy said. "They're about a hundred years too late for that."

"Let's set up the Bren," Harry ordered. "Hans, do you smoke?"

"Yah."

"Timothy, give the man a cigarette. We're friends now," Harry ordered. "Hans, you're to protect Tim and me with that Karabiner of yours."

"You're in charge," Hans agreed.

Harry talked as he knocked down some of the fence stones to make a cradle for the Bren. A bolt shattered on a rock with a loud crack, knocking if off the wall to his side.

"What rank are you?"

"Lieutenant."

Harry laughed. Of course an officer had ran. "Not anymore. You're a private now, or you're a prisoner if you have a problem with that. If we get out of this, I'll see you get fair treatment. I'm in charge here, you work for me."

"Yah," Hans agreed again.

"The rest of you men, spread out along the wall. There's a lot more of them than us, but they don't have guns. Don't be stupid, those crossbows are going to be every bit as deadly. So when I say, we open up with what we have. When you're out of all ammo except your pistol, run to the Matador, and get ready to leave. When we must, we'll go, and fast. There will be no shame."

"We have bayonets, Sergeant."

"Wilkes, if I see you using a bayonet on these guys, I'll shoot you myself. There are fifteen of us, not one a hero. You heard my order."

Wilkes didn't answer, but looked relieved. Let the Spitfire pilots be brave. Harry realized how desperately he wanted to survive this and get home to his wife.

The sound of clanking iron echoed off the treeline and up the hill.

"Fire at will!" Harry bellowed as Timothy slapped a magazine into the now ready Bren gun.

The sounds of battle erupted. True to his word, Hans worked as a sniper with his accurate rifle, targeting any crossbowman that looked like he was aiming at the machine gun emplacement. The melee infantry of the enemy, mostly carrying axes, began marching up the hill.

The smaller caliber weapons, like the Lee Enfield rifles carried by most of Harry's men, proved to be ineffective against the strange armor worn by this new enemy. Even the Bren, firing the .303 cartridge like the Enfields, failed to directly penetrate the black armor. Harry found that by concentrating bursts on one soldier, that soldier would be bowled over by the energy of the attack and often roll back down the incline, sometimes taking others along for the ride.

Still, there was no way that was going to win the battle. The only gun they had that was at all effective was Han's Kar98k, and even it only occasionally penetrated.

When Harry'd heard the fourth of his men die under attack from the crossbows, he'd seen enough. "Get to the Matador," he yelled. "We're abandoning our position."

"What about Harris? Mattison?"

"Leave them. We won't die for the dead today," Harry ordered.

He knew his behaviors might well get him a firing squad. There were still those who thought dying at the hands of a superior enemy was better than fleeing.

Harry didn't see it that way. He had reason to make it home, and not as a lifeless body.

He and Tim grabbed their Bren, not that it was of much use. He jumped into the passenger seat of the vehicle as the rest of the men dove into the back. "Hans, you're up front. Middle."

To his relief, the Matador started, and they turned quickly to race away from the wall.

Four of his men had died, bolts through their skulls.

That left him eleven.

Plus Hans, so for now, twelve. Despite the war, he'd keep Hans for now. With things unfolding like this, who knew what was going to happen, he wasn't about to leave the German alone in the wilderness. Maybe he'd get Hans a British uniform if the Dunkirk evacuation was called off and they stayed on the continent. If things got crazy enough.

A bolt from a crossbow punched through the back of the lorry's cab, shattering the front left window as it exited.

It had probably missed Harry by four inches.

He hoped the men in the bed were alright, but it wasn't any sort of time to stop and see.

"Keep driving, Wilkes. As fast as you can without shaking the men back there out," he said gesturing toward the rear.

They drove for several minutes, then Wilkes slowed down.

Harry leaned out of the window and opened the front edge of the canvas canopy on the lorry's bed. "Everyone make it?"

"That one that went through the cab was the only shot that hit us, Harry," Tim answered. "No damage back here, but glad to see you didn't snuff it."

"Not yet," Harry replied as he pulled the fabric closed.

He sat back in his seat and thought of the battle for a moment.

"Where can I get more of those K98s?" he asked the German.

"I doubt you'll talk anyone into giving theirs up," Hans said. "You'll have to take them, or find stouter guns of your own."

Harry nodded, not that Hans could probably tell with the way the Matador was bouncing across the landscape.

He'd find adequate guns.

Because he wasn't going to fight without them.

Several minutes later they passed the burning debris of a Spitfire in a freshly planted wheat field. The cockpit was ripped open, by what looked like claws.

"Gott have mercy," Hans said.

"If he did, this wouldn't have happened in the first place," Harry said, aware of the bitterness in his tone.

Hans said nothing in reply.

Which was for the best.

Chapter 7 - Earth

Irsu's platoon stood in front of the gate. Behind him was the rest of his brother's company, ready to follow the lead platoon into the breach between worlds.

"If this doesn't make your iron brittle, nothing will," Coragg said.

"I was thinking of a more personal symptom of the experience," Irsu replied, tapping the plate over his groin. "I can tell you right now that if our ancestors hadn't agreed to this madness, I'd be headin' the other way."

"Too late now," Coragg sighed. "And ancestors are watching. My granpaps is probably shaking his head as fast as I'm shaking my knees."

Irsu laughed. "Is that what that tapping sound is?"

Coragg grinned. They joked about being afraid, but if there were a way out at this point, they'd not take it. It was their way, as friends, to speak of their emotions when they would to few others.

Irsu turned to his dwarves. "Hearthfire platoon is the strongest and hottest of the flames in Iron Company. We are first of our kin. We are first to see this new place. We, Hearthfire, we brave the magic next."

Nobody cheered. The dwarven warriors facing him lowered their visors and gripped their axes at the ready.

Hagirr stood on a small platform near the gate. Turning to look at the dwarves, it felt as if he were staring into Irsu's soul. "Dwarves of the Iron Mountains, you're next. That first small unit, march through the gate."

"Who's he callin' small?" Coragg grumbled.

"Forward," Irsu bellowed to his platoon.

As one the unit stepped off with their left foot, followed by the right in unison. It made a martial sound, the iron greaves of the Hearthfire platoon marching toward their fate. Behind them the other three platoons of Iron Company started singing.

Their people had waited ten thousand years for this. And only seconds of that stretch of time remained.

As they reached the glowing barrier between worlds, the dwarves didn't hesitate. Irsu marched through first, and Coragg right behind him, then his forty soldiers in two lines. Passing the barrier was remarkably without sensation. Only the texture of the ground beneath his feet changed over the course of a nearly blind twenty steps.

Then he passed into a world alive with sounds. At first it reminded Irsu of the forges in his home community, the great hammers flattening out metals into usable sheets.

Then something terrifying flew over them, with a roar unlike any beast he'd ever heard. Moments later the ground around him, strewn with rubble and charred black with fire, erupted in tiny splatters of anger as another of the flying beasts spat death down toward his unit. He looked up at the sky, wondering which way was north.

"Ready your crossbows," he barked as his soldiers appeared behind him. "There is danger from the sky here."

The two that had flown so near him before were off to his right, either the east and the rising sun or the west and the setting sun. He'd know which soon enough.

"Two ranks, prepare to fire if they come around again," he ordered.

The dwarves created a north-south line facing the creature, in two ranks. The front rank kneeled down and raised their crossbows, braced against the ground with their axes.

Those shots would be accurate. The rear rank held their crossbows up by hand, firing over the heads of their fellows. They'd be less accurate. But sometimes inaccuracy helps account for unexpected movements by the enemy.

The creatures groaned in the distance as they swung around to attack Irsu's unit. At that very moment the first dwarves of the next platoon, Anvil platoon, walked through into the new world.

"We're under attack from the sky," Irsu bellowed at his fellow platoon leader. Seek cover, the creatures spit tiny darts. Lots of 'em."

As Anvil platoon sought shelter, the creatures lined up on Irsu's soldiers once more. Fire spat from orifices on the front of the creature's unflapping wings, and a second later the dirt in front of his unit once again exploded in tiny columns. The second creature repeated the actions of the first.

"FIRE!" Irsu screamed at the same time as some of his unit grunted with shock.

Six of his soldiers fell to the ground, bowled over by the force of the creature's dart attack.

A horrendous sound, much like the rending of any metal, occurred behind his line. A ball of fire rose into the air, burning with orange and black styrations. One of the creatures was on the ground, the other raced off into the sky in the direction they'd originally come from.

Four of the six stricken dwarves got up, with massive dents in their armor. As they did so the next platoon came through the gate. Granite Platoon.

"We'll have to get somewhere safe to hammer that out," he said to the first man he helped up. "Until then, get a backup from the reserve stores when the wagons come through with Iron Platoon."

The young dwarf nodded, picked up his crossbow and axe, wincing in pain as the dented armor pressed against what were probably broken ribs.

Whatever those flying creatures were, they packed a punch.

"Help the others, Coragg. See to them as you can," Irsu said. "You two," he said, pointing at the two nearest soldiers. "You're with me. Let's see this creature for ourselves."

As they approached, it became clear it wasn't a creature at all.

But a machine.

Fire burned furiously around it. Waves of heat distorted his vision of the thing, but he could see well enough to see what had brought it down. A burning human sat inside it, probably in control of the machine prior to his death. A flying machine. How interesting. When the gnomes came through, probably at the end, they'd want to examine devices such as this one. Irsu hoped there were plenty of them to fight. War is no fun if it's not a challenge, and humans were historically considered even weaker than elves.

He stared through the shimmering heat, to see the human. Charred, but he could clearly see a bolt sticking through the man's head and into the seat behind him.

One of his dwarves had shot the fellow in the face.

A few minutes through the gate and they'd already killed an enemy. The Underking would need to hear it, in time. His platoon would be honored, something they deserved.

His brother greeted him as he got back to his unit.

"Coragg says you were examining the beast that did this?"

"Twas no beast, but a machine."

"A flying machine?"

"The dragon said as much, but you can't believe it until you see it," Irsu assured Bordnu.

"Two are dead," Coragg said, walking up to the brothers. "At this rate we'll be expended soon."

"We know now," Irsu said. "Our soldiers died to show us, so that our kin might live. No greater honor."

"No greater honor," Bordnu and Coragg replied in unison.

"Get what you need from the wagons," Bordnu ordered, clasping Irsu's shoulder. Put your unit's damaged armors in storage. Once we reach a lull, we'll repair."

Irsu nodded. "On your feet," he barked at his soldiers. "These humans aren't going to kill themselves." He picked out his two strongest. "You and you. Get the fallen into the wagons. Better the supply train pull them than we carry them."

"Aye," both of them agreed. They knew that if the dead needed carried, they'd be the ones doing it. And Iron Mountain dwarves did not leave the dead behind if it could be helped. The ancestors wouldn't tolerate it.

"Which way is east?" Bordnu asked him.

"Hells if I know," Irsu replied. "That way or that one."

"Then find cover. We wait until the sun rises toward or falls from the horizon."

"Great idea," Irsu said. "Must be all those learning scrolls you read."

Bordnu made a rude gesture and walked off toward his own unit.

"You were planning just that, I saw you looking at the sky," Coragg said after Bordnu was gone.

"Let him think he's the smart one. It's plain to see I got the looks. He needs something."

They laughed as they formed into ranks once again, and for the first time in ten thousand years the sound of Iron Mountain dwarves marching echoed in the air of Earth.

As they waited Irsu stood by the wagon that held his dead comrades.

These were the first losses he'd experienced as a commander.

He voiced a silent prayer to Mordain to accept them into the sky.

Chapter 8 - Saved by Necessity

May 23, 1940

Ernst looked down at the desk in front of him.

A Luger sat on the wood surface, grimly reminding him of the reality of what happened at Rotterdam. The safety was off.

Field Marshal Gerd von Rundstedt, commander of the Panzer Divisions assigned to roll through France, sat on the other side of the desk with the fingertips of both hands touching in front of him.

Ernst took that as a sign of contemplation.

Maybe he wasn't to be shot after all.

"Your device, and the effects, Herr Haufmann, is causing no end of problems to the Führer's plans for Western Europe."

"I understand this," Ernst replied. "The missions to Finland, Nepal, and then the task at Rotterdam were all approved at the highest levels." He couldn't say that Hitler himself had not only approved the collection of the artifacts, but the deployment. Blaming the Führer would be the quickest way to the firing squad.

"Because you told the High Command the result would be a weapon usable against the allies," von Rundstedt replied. The Field Marshall's voice didn't have even the slightest edge of anger to it.

Maybe Ernst would be shot.

"Do you believe in the German cause?" the Field Marshall asked Ernst.

"Do I? I have sacrificed everything for it. I am a paragon of loyalty."

"Then one last sacrifice," von Rundstedt said, picking the pistol up by the barrel and gesturing for Ernst to take it. "You deserve the dignity of ending your own life, since I believe you were trying to do good for the Fatherland."

Ernst took the pistol. For a brief moment he considered shooting his superior and running. But there were guards all over the estate house they were in. Even if he killed von Rundstedt, he wouldn't get far. And the SS would come for his mother, and his brothers and sisters, assuming them to be traitors as well.

He was left with no choice.

He looked at von Rundstedt, smiled, then raised the pistol to his head.

"Heil, Hitler," Ernst said before pulling the trigger.

The gun clicked, but nothing happened.

"So you are loyal. Good. Then I can trust you will fix the mess you have created," von Rundstedt said, standing up. "Nobody other than you and Meckler have the knowledge needed. And neither you nor I know where Meckler is." He shrugged. "I needed to see you were a man of honor for myself."

Ernst dropped the gun on the desk. "Some would say that to put a man through such a test is not itself honorable, Field Marshall."

"We're at war. There is no time for subtlety."

Ernst understood that at least. "What will you have me do?"

"Whatever it takes. You will select a dozen people for your team. Scientists, theologians, or whatever you need. No more than a dozen. No less. Twenty-four Waffen-SS troops will be assigned to guard, and if need be work for you."

That was bigger than his old squad, even before most of them didn't make it out of Rotterdam.

"And, if need be, shoot me I am sure," Ernst said.

"You are a very bold and outspoken man," von Rundstedt replied. "I have yet to decide if I like it. Fortunately, your knowledge leaves me no choice but to tolerate it."

Ernst didn't answer. Maybe he was antagonizing the officer too much.

"For now," the Field Marshall finished. He walked to the door, opened it, and barked orders to an attendant. "We're executing plan B in regard to Herr Haufmann."

"Why do you not call me Oberstleutnant?" Ernst asked.

"Because you no longer serve in the military ranks," von Rundstedt said. "A decision I agree with, since you seem naturally insubordinate. You are, until this matter is resolved at the very least, Herr Haufmann, a civilian contractor for the Third Reich, and Director of the Ahnenerbe program."

That was a shock. He'd spent many years rising to his rank, and while it might be true he questioned authority, it was only because he was so often more intelligent than those who commanded him.

Maybe he would be better off as a civilian.

"But I still command this task force to shut the Interna Hojarr down?"

"You do."

"Then I will get started picking my staff," Ernst said. "With your leave."

Field Marshall von Rundstedt abruptly walked back toward his desk, an obvious gesture of dismissal. "Goodbye, Herr Haufmann."

"Good day to you, Field Marshall."

Ernst walked through the offices to leave, marveling at his good fortune. It was a good thing Meckler disappeared, or the leadership might have considered Ernst more expendable.

That wouldn't do. Not at all.

He would be careful not to share all the relevant details of his craft with anyone ever again.

Chapter 9 - Churchill

May 23, 1940

Harry's fire team rested near Arras after retreating from Roeselare.

For several days nothing happened. Britain had a new Prime Minister, and nobody knew what that meant. The German advance had stopped, and nobody knew quite how to deal with that either.

Rumors abounded. Some rumors said the Germans were moving their troops north to fight the undying soldiers of Satan and the End Times War had begun. Still others said that God had sent the monsters to fight on Britain's side, because He was going to actually save the Queen.

Harry didn't buy any of that drivel. He'd seen the enemy, and while terrifying in their near invulnerability, his team had killed a few.

The problem was very few believed him. One officer had even accused Harry's team of cowardice, and only Timothy rapidly grabbing Harry's arms had saved that officer from a flattening he'd remember.

They hadn't seen Hans in a day, he was being interrogated by the brass. Harry'd hoped to keep the German a secret, honestly, but there'd been no way to do it. At least the powers that be hadn't shipped him off immediately to a cell in a prison camp. They wouldn't as long as they thought Hans had useful information.

Hans had also backed up Harry's story, and that of all the men in his unit. He owed the German for that, but truth be told he'd probably saved Han's life back at Roeselare, so maybe they were even.

"The new Prime Minister is on the wireless," someone yelled from inside a nearby tent.

Harry stopped at the tent and listened from the doorway as two dozen others gathered inside. Even with everyone around, he could have heard a pin drop.

An announcer spoke first. "The Prime Minister was to speak to us all a few days ago, but stories of strange news from the front has pushed back his speech to now according to officials reporting from 10 Downing Street. Ladies and Gentlemen, the Prime Minister."

A slight delay as the speakers switched in some distant unseen location.

"I speak to you for the first time as Prime Minister in a solemn hour for the life of our country, of our empire, of our allies, and, above all, of the cause of freedom. A tremendous battle is raging in France and Flanders. The Germans, by a remarkable combination of air bombing and heavily armored tanks, have broken through the French defenses north of the Maginot Line, and strong columns of their armored vehicles are ravaging the open country, which for the first day or two was without defenders. They have penetrated deeply and spread alarm and confusion in their track. Behind them there are now appearing infantry in lorries, and behind them, again, the large masses are moving forward. The re-groupment of the French armies to make head against, and also to strike at, this intruding wedge has been proceeding for several days, largely assisted by the magnificent efforts of the Royal Air Force.

"All that said, we do not know where the battle stands at this time. Reports of supernatural events in Belgium have sprung up, although very little has been confirmed by your government. Whether this is as a result of some German atrocity, or whether God himself has decided to punish the wickedness of Man, we do not know. What we hear are mostly rumors so spectacular they are hardly to be believed."

"You better believe it, Prime Minister," Harry whispered.

"Ssshhh," the man next to him scolded.

Harry shrugged and went back to listening.

"—whatever the state of affairs in Flanders, we, as a people, have the righteous strength of freedom on our side. We have the morality of that righteousness, and as such we will find our way to the correct and just answers in regards to this matter. At this moment, we simply do not know enough to tell you what is happening. Maybe once we rescue more of our boys from the continent, they'll have a more clear story to tell."

That fired the men in the tent up a bit. They were more than eager to share the peculiar things they'd seen.

"You blokes shut it!" someone near the radio snapped.

Everyone got quiet again.

"It's important we remember, today is Trinity Sunday. Centuries ago words were written to be a call and a spur to the faithful servants of truth and justice: *Arm yourselves, and be ye men of valor, and be in readiness for the conflict; for it is better for us to perish in battle than to look upon the outrage of our nation and our altars. As the will of God is in Heaven, even so let it be.*"

A pause, then the original voice. "This has been a public announcement from your Prime Minister. Back to our programming."

With that the radio returned to playing music.

Harry walked away, heading toward his squad's tent.

"Did you listen to Churchill, Sergeant?" one of his men asked as he entered.

"I did. He knows less than we do, which is saying a lot about how in the dark that man is."

A few men laughed.

"More to matters, what is the plan for us?" a different one asked. "We fled our post, never made it to our assigned spot."

"We're off the hook, thanks to Hans," Harry said. "He backed up our story, as he should, it was the bloody truth."

Mumbles of agreement mixed with a few words of regret for their lost brothers.

"We need to work on picking up more serious guns," Harry said. "I still have Han's Karabiner, but only seven rounds for it."

"What options we got?" Timothy asked. "Lee-Enfields and Bren's about it, right?"

"There's a bunch of French guns down at the depot," Wilkes said. "Hotchkisses, some rifles. All bigger caliber than we got."

"And how many times have those been dropped?" Timothy asked.

Laughter.

"But they're like new, they've never been fired!" another soldier said.

More laughter.

It was good to see his men feeling brotherhood.

"Did you hear that before this lull in the fighting a French Field Commander was trying to get his government to surrender early?"

"Just a rumor, private, let's not spread nonsense," Harry ordered. "We have to work with the Frogs. There's plenty of them brave as any of us. They just got a history of their generals pissing themselves."

Laughter again.

"Tell me about those guns, Wilkes," Harry said.

"Some of the Hotchkisses are 11mm, some are 7.92, which is what the Karabiner is although it's not the same round. You don't want to mix them up," Wilkes said. "The rifles are 7.5mm, so probably almost as good as Han's gun. Anyone know if the round is high velocity?"

"Better than what we have," Timothy said. "Can we get our hands on them?"

"They're for us to use if we want, just nobody wants. We get ours, then after we're set we explain why. That way we have first pick," Harry said. "I want ammo for a siege."

"How much?"

"As much as we can comfortably carry and then a touch past that," Harry said. "Plus get some cases to put in our lorry. I don't think we're going home for a while."

Groans.

"Did you expect we would? Dragons are eating Spitfires, short men in armor are killing squads of soldiers on both sides of the war, and you thought we'd just pack it up?" Harry said, angry.

Nobody answered him.

He didn't expect one. "Get the guns, Wilkes. Take a couple of these bell ends with you to carry gear. If you see AP rounds, grab those. Those black iron wearing bastards won't know what happened if we have some real firepower."

"On it, Sergeant."

"Hurry. Something's going to break soon. I feel it."

He watched Wilkes head out. As he closed the door, it started to rain. He rushed to the flap and looked up. It had been blue skies when he entered the tent moments before. Now towering thunderheads formed a line heading off into the distance and fat heavy drops hit the dusty soil at his feet.

Lightning crashed not too far away.

Ominous, but maybe a good thing. Could dragons fly during such storms?

He'd know the answer soon, most likely.

Chapter 10 - Hans

May 23, 1940

Somehow being guarded in a tent and questioned a hundred times in a day wasn't what he'd expected when he surrendered to the British near Roeselare.

They weren't treating him bad, and honestly, he couldn't say he had the same hopes for British prisoners taken by the SS or even regular German troops. The Wermacht, particular the Heer, were whipped into a frenzy of conquest by the political propaganda of Goebbels and his Ministry.

Hans, and most intelligent men in the Heer, had never bought into that. The Germans were men, just like the British, the French, or the Americans. When the war started, he'd been every bit as excited for German victory as any other soldier, but for different reasons than many of the Nazi party members.

He wasn't fighting for German superiority, but for German equality. The Treaty of Versailles had robbed Germany of wealth, of opportunity, and of dignity. It was time to fix that.

He'd had no idea how successful Rommel's panzers would be in breaking through the Maginot and steamrolling France. Once that had happened, the delusion of German superiority swelled to even greater heights among Han's peers.

Then something had happened in Rotterdam, although Hans had no idea what that something was. As a result of Rotterdamn, terrible creatures had poured from the city, slaughtering civilians, Belgian troops, German troops, and, as he learned after his surrender, Allied troops.

There was a new enemy on the field, one that he feared would conclusively prove Germany's superiority was fictional. The price of that proof might be the destruction of humanity.

The flap of his tent opened, and a British officer looked in. "Get ready, Colonel Hamlin will see you in fifteen minutes."

"What am I to say that I have not already said?" Hans asked.

"Mate, only you know that."

The officer closed the flap, and Hans reached for his boots. Sergeant Hughes, who he'd surrendered to, had promised him fair treatment. Which he'd gotten. But maybe it was a mistake to surrender. Maybe he should have made his way back to German lines alone and reunited with the Heer. At least German rifles could harm the enemy. The British seemed wholly ineffective.

It was raining, he heard the sound on his tent. He donned his helmet as it was all he had to protect himself from the downpour. It was likely to be a wicked storm judging by the sound of the land covering rumbles from nearby lightning strikes.

Clothed, he opened the flap to see one of the guards outside. "I'm ready," he announced.

"Come on then," the guard said, grabbing Hans roughly by the arm. "And hurry. I am already tired of being wet. Where I'm taking you, there is a roof."

As they left, Hans saw guards all around his tent. A dozen men to keep him locked in, even though he'd willingly surrendered and told the British everything he knew about the real enemy, which was whatever was coming out of Rotterdam. He'd not betrayed the secrets of his own army, but then everything he knew about their positions or intentions was almost certainly outdated by now.

The introduction of a new enemy and front in the war would force Herr Hitler to change, or at least delay, his plans for the conquest of Europe.

"Quit stalling," the guard said, and jerked Hans by the arm although Hans wasn't stalling at all.

A few meters ahead of them the ground rippled.

The guard stopped, confused by the phenomenon.

Hans did the same, puzzled.

A dozen meters to the right, the ground rippled in a different spot.

"What the damnation?" the guard asked nobody in particular.

Almost simultaneously the ground erupted upward in both spots. Around him he heard other similar disturbances as well.

Then the screams began.

A creature stood before him, one that had once been a man. Skeletal, it had some tissue regrowing over the bones at an unbelievably fast rate. A second creature stood at the other ripple, but it ran into a nearby tent. Sounds of men dying in hideous fashion followed.

An eyeball popped into existence as the remaining creature whipped its head around to face the guard and Hans.

As a trachea formed in front of the bare spine of the neck, a low groan erupted from the skeleton become beast.

It leapt on the guard, who shrieked going down. The bones of the creature's hands sank into the guard's flesh, and as Hans stood frozen he saw life blood flow upward from the man's punctured body onto the bones of the monster.

Where blood flowed over bone, new tissue began to grow.

The plaintive cries of the guard brought Hans back to the moment, and although he'd recoiled a few meters when the attack started, he now ran forward to grab the man's pistol, which had fallen on the dirt.

Hans put three rounds into the chest of the foul thing, which seemed to have absolutely no effect. As the beast ripped more violently into its victim, bodily fluids were flowing upward onto the bones of the creature with great rapidity. As blood drained from the guard, the creature was using it to repair any damage Hans did faster than the damage could be done.

Hans leveled the pistol at the creature's brain case and pulled the trigger.

The roar as the gun fired seemed simultaneous with the creature collapsing on top of the guard, partially formed fingers still embedded in the stricken Brit's mangled torso.

Hans kicked the creature off to the side, and then knelt down to see to the guard's condition.

Just in time to look into the eyes of a dying man.

There was fear there, fear of something Hans couldn't see.

Then there was nothing.

A shudder tore through Hans, caused by what he'd seen in his dead captor's eyes. For a moment he remained frozen in horror even as the sounds of devastation echoed through the British encampment.

"Hans?"

He looked up. It was Wilkes, one of Harry's men. Wilkes was a man who possessed some common sense, and Hans somewhat liked as much as one could like a captor. Two other men were with him, all three were carrying an assortment of rifle, machine guns, and ammunition.

"Private Wilkes, you're alive. That's good to see."

"We've no time for that," Wilkes said. "Come with me if you want to live."

"Where?" Hans asked even as he rose to comply. He shoved his newly acquired pistol into his belt. These creatures could be ended with a bullet, and there was no way he'd agree to be disarmed again.

"Harry's at the tent. He'll be happy to have you with us if you're of a mind to do so."

"Let's go," Hans said, offering to take part of Wilkes' load.

"I'll carry, you shoot anything in our way that isn't human," Wilkes said. His eyes glanced toward the ground. "Apparently you know where to shoot."

"I think I do. I'll follow your lead."

The four men made their way a hundred meters along a line of tents, as they did so an infantry lorry came screaming into the camp. It stopped near them and two men jumped out, one of them heavily wounded with a tear to the flesh of his arm.

"Where's the commander?" one asked.

"No idea, what's happening?" Wilkes asked in return.

"Arras Memorial, it's…" He stopped as if he didn't believe what he had to say.

"What?" Wilkes demanded.

"The dead, they live again," the man replied as he moved to hold up his comrade. "We don't have enough bullets for this."

The men turned to find someone else who might know where the camp's commander was.

"Wait," Hans said.

The Brit turned to look at him, seemingly noticing his German uniform for the first time. "What in bloody Hell?"

"The commandant's office is that way, four hundred meters," Hans informed him. "A one-story farm house. You will not miss it if you go that way."

The soldier, who Han at first worried might drop his friend and attack him, instead dropped the hostility from his face. "We'll take this then," he said, resignation in his voice as he helped his friend back into the vehicle. "It will be quicker."

"Come on, lad," Wilkes urged Hans. "We need to get to the boys."

Hans followed him again. Soon they were inside the unit's tent, after passing four of Harry's men standing guard outside. None of the men even blinked at seeing Hans.

Inside the tent smelled of blood and fear.

"It's you!" Harry said, clasping the German by the shoulder. "Good job, Wilkes, you've helped me keep my word."

"They can be killed," Hans replied. "I did so."

"I know." Harry pointed at a pile in the corner, a pile of bones and malformed human flesh. "That one rose up right under Jenkin's cot."

"That explains the smell in here," Hans said.

Harry only nodded as he started passing out the guns Wilkes had secured. "Well done, Wilkes! We have enough ammo for some time."

The private beamed under the praise of the sergeant. Hans could see Harry was still effective as a leader, despite all the strange goings on.

"We'll need to get away from whatever is causing this," Harry said, waving toward the corpse. "We may need to fight our way out of the camp."

"It's all the WWI soldiers buried here where they fell," Timothy said. "I'd wager my next meal it's associated with the strange things we've seen this week."

"That's absurd," someone said.

Gunfire from outside accentuated Timothy's claim.

"You deny your own eyes," Tim said to his heckler. "Not a good move if you want to live."

"Can't wager what you don't know you'll have, Tim, but I agree," Harry said. "Something is bringing the dead back, and they're not fighting on our side."

Harry handed Hans his Karabiner. "You can have this, there are still seven rounds. Or you can take one of the French MAS-36s Wilkes got us."

"I'll take both if there is enough," Hans said. The Kar98K was comfort. But seven rounds was a problem. The MAS would be his backup, his new British friends had thousands of rounds for those.

"Everyone load up," Harry ordered. "Timothy and I will take the Hotchkiss along with rifles. Everyone will carry one canister of the 11mm ammo for the machine gun. If we meet more of those armored chaps, we'll need plenty."

Two minutes later they were all armed, even the four men outside who were the source of many of the shots they heard. The bodies of the dead lay about, along with a few Brit soldiers from other squads.

"Let's get to the lorries and get our Matador," Harry ordered. "Hans, you're in back this time. Put your rifle skills to work."

"Yah," Hans replied. "I just want to get out of this alive."

Harry nodded at him in agreement. "Depends on how many of the dead are rising, and how well they stand up to being run over by a three-ton lorry, I suppose."

"We should go find out."

Harry picked up the Hotchkiss to carry as he ran. "Let's do that."

Chapter 11 - Hell, Hitler

May 23, 1940

"The Führer has been assassinated," the field radio blared.

Ernst was surprised to see such openness about the event. The Nazis weren't exactly forthcoming with information for the most part. That meant the release of this information had an unseen goal that would satisfy the killers of Herr Hitler.

What could that goal be?

"Generals Franz Halder and Walther von Brauchitsch have been arrested following the assassination, any and all officials related closely to the two generals are to be arrested on sight. A list of potential conspirators will be forwarded to all front-line field offices."

Who was in power now?

Ernst hated such unpredictability. He was well under way with picking staff for his research team, many of them were already being delivered to Bad Münstereifel, where Ernst would assemble them into what he needed.

Disorder at the top of the German command structure would only frustrate his requests for supplies and any additional staff.

On the list of things he needed were several occult artifacts that were only rumored to exist. The Ark of the Covenant being one, although it was most likely to be real of all the items on his list. Ernst believed the Ark to be far more than the icon of faith the religious idiots who claimed to harbor it did. In his opinion it was the Ark that separated the Earth from other worlds like the one intruding on it now.

Something about the Intepna Hojarr, however, had pierced that protection.

Ernst felt the solution was to bring the Ark closer to the breach, and with that proximity whatever protective field emanated from the Ark would be powerful enough to seal the breech.

That was his first plan.

He was still letting a backup plan coalesce in his mind. The one that kept popping into his mind was "flee to Switzerland", which wasn't a valid solution. If whoever was Führer now continued to prosecute the war, it was only a matter of time before the Swiss too were brought into the Reich. After all, Germans everywhere deserved to be under a German banner.

For now, plan A would do. He'd assemble his team and get closer to the breach, to see if there was an obvious way to close it. If not, his team would go to Ethiopia and secure the Ark if it existed there.

Tomorrow most of the occult specialists he needed would arrive. He had a transport plane waiting nearby, his team would fly over the breach if that was possible. Take images. Then bring them back here where they'd brainstorm a plan.

He looked at the open book on his desk. Open to a page displaying an artist's rendition of the Ark of the Covenant. It didn't look like it would be hard to steal, if the depiction was accurate, it seemed two men could pick it up like a litter and just walk away with it.

If that were so why hadn't it been stolen before?

He'd need experts to determine that as well.

Why was life so complicated? It was easier for the religious. They got to blame everything on their God, or their Devil. For him, the best he could hope for was for someone else to take the blame for any mistakes he made.

Meckler had already paid a price higher than Ernst wished to pay and was no longer available to be Ernst's scapegoat.

He'd need to find another.

Chapter 12 - Resistance

"So, there are several human factions?" Coragg asked as they marched. "Why not let them kill each other and save our soldiers for the cleanup?"

"They're pathetic at it. Their slug spitters aren't worth the metal in them," Irsu scoffed. "We need to engage, or they'll breed faster than they die."

Several warriors around laughed.

Over the last several days the Iron Company had attacked four different units of humans, all in dark gray uniforms. One unit had prisoners from a different human faction, wearing brown uniforms. Bordnu had ordered those humans set free and given them a scroll with directions on it.

Irsu had protested, but Bordnu overruled him, saying that the effect on the enemy when they got the scroll would be worth a few humans surviving the engagement.

Later, marching with his platoon, Irsu had a thought.

"It occurs to me, Coragg." Irsu raised his face plate and scratched his nose. "Do you think the humans can read stonescript?"

Coragg raised his visor, stared at Irsu, then chuckled. "No, of course not. Why didn't anyone think of that before?"

Irsu shook his head and hefted his axe higher on his shoulder. "We won't make that mistake again."

They marched several hours, until the sun sat low in the west. There were plenty of roads, but the company avoided them. They moved across the countryside, and where possible, through forests. Several times over the last days they had to make rafts to cross streams. The latest terrain the dwarves marched across was rolling hills dotted with fertile fields. Slowly the hills grew higher and Irsu knew that mountainous terrain was ahead somewhere.

Ahead of them was a small country farm, lit with the bright and unseemly torches the humans used. They couldn't see in the dark, but does that mean they needed to banish it as an enemy? Hardly, but that's what they did. It was hard to even see the stars.

The dwarves of Iron Company spread out

A strange vehicle pulled into the grounds ahead of them, let onto the property by a group of the gray soldiers who guarded the fencing and the gate. Strange wire with razors on it wove around the wood of the fence and would make crossing the barrier hard for anyone not wearing armor.

The ugly four-armed waterwheel flag fluttered over the front of the house on a pole.

"That razor wire is a great idea," Coragg said. "We should carry that idea back to our homes with us."

Irsu grunted. "Useless against armor."

"But perfect for thieves and spies."

"Good point," Irsu conceded. "Get some if you can, after we take this place."

"We attack then?"

"Why not? Bordnu will decide, but he won't want to leave any enemies behind us who might find our trail. It's not like you're not leaving footprints, you fat oaf."

"Food is good," Coragg said in tacit agreement with the fat remark. "I hope they have something good to eat inside, if we're going to take this place."

Bordnu tapped Irsu on the shoulder. "When my platoon charges, we all charge. There are two fortifications with the heavier spitter sticks that can penetrate our armor. One is just north of the house, the other is south. Your platoon will destroy the north one."

"And the humans inside the building? They must be important to be so well guarded. Do we take them?"

"They are of no use to us," was all Bordnu had to say before he disappeared back into the dark. Iron company had polished armor, and in the darkness under the light of Earth's large moon it danced with streaks of light. The effect was almost magical in appearance.

Moments later Bordnu's platoon charged toward the front gate with a war scream. Irsu pushed through the brush shielding his unit from view, then screamed his rage at the enemy. Hearthstone platoon rushed across a small field to the fence, arriving just as the enemy opened fire with their spitter sticks.

"Coragg, get this fence down," Irsu ordered.

"Aye," his second answered as he tossed his pack on the ground to remove tools.

"Crossbows!" he barked to his soldiers. "Suppress the spitter sticks!"

Just as he finished the order, the nested spitter stick Bordnu had mentioned opened fire on the fence row. Several of his soldiers grunted as they were knocked off their feet, he noticed two of them not struggling to get up. That made him angry. These were his brothers in arms.

He unstrapped his crossbow as his archers fired their first volley at the enemy.

The heavy spitter silenced for a moment, then started back up again, and more of his platoon fell.

He set his axe into the ground, then leveled the crossbow on the hilt of the axe. The two weapons were designed to work together as a firing platform and base. He stuck a dagger blade into the pulley for the bow string, pulling it back into position until it clicked. He placed a quarrel given him by a priest while he was still at Iron Mountain into the breach of the weapon.

"Ixtithius," he muttered, and the bolt came alive with a red glow.

Even as the ground erupted around him with more spitter fire, he carefully aimed at the flames the heavy spitter emitted. Then he fired.

The quarrel lanced across the field, a red streak flying straight and true to the target. Irsu couldn't tell exactly what it hit, but it didn't matter. A sphere of red light erupted from the impact point, as wide as a full-grown cave bear could stretch. Everything inside the light began to smoke, and the screams began. The humans operating the spitter writhed as their skin began to boil from their bodies, their uniforms catching on fire as well.

The bolt wasn't done. The heat continued to rise, until the spitter itself exploded due to the fire powder the human weapons used.

The light blinked out as orange hot slag that had been the human weapon drooped to the ground, centered in a circle of glowing dirt turned to glass. No trace of the humans remained, having been turned to carbon.

"By the beard of the Underking, how many of those do you have?" Coragg asked.

"That was one of three," Irsu said. "Worth spending seeing as we were dying."

"Aye," Coragg agreed. "Spend one sooner next time."

As other humans with portable spitter sticks attacked, the dwarven crossbows picked them off. Soon the field near the house seemed covered with bodies, and the field by the fence as well.

"I'm through this infernal wire," Coragg told him.

"We go in, but we've done our part. Bordnu gave us a target, and we took it out."

"We're done fighting?"

"No, but we're done sticking our heads up." Irsu turned to his soldiers. "Agits, Norgrin, get the wounded lined up by the fence here," he ordered, his arms sweeping out an area for them to use. "Put the dead in a stack over there. We'll put them on wagons when the carts show up."

The two soldiers snapped to their duties.

"The rest of you, we're headed to the house. Another lesson learned at an absurd price. We'll need to be more cautious against the spitter nests."

They pushed through the broken fence line and headed to the still lit house. Bordnu's unit had pushed through the front gate after killing everyone there. His brother met him near the front door of the house.

"Losses?" Bordnu asked.

"Several."

"Their spirits will join the ancestors. Let's get inside."

Bordnu kicked the front door in, a human inside had a spitter that fit in one hand. He shot it at Bordnu until it clicked, none of the slugs from it penetrated his brother's stout armor.

A swift swing of his axe, and Bordnu took the human down at the legs. Another swing stopped the screaming.

Scrambling toward the back of the house alerted Irsu to more humans. He rushed through an open archway to see a girl and a boy. Both were young, prior to breeding age.

Bordnu stepped up behind Irsu. "Step aside. They're of no use to us."

"We don't kill children," Irsu said.

"We don't leave anyone that can report on us either," Bordnu replied.

"They are young and will not be of any use reporting our mission. I demand their lives be spared."

Bordnu stared at him, then finally grunted. "The risk is great. The price is on your shoulders."

"No price greater than my soul would pay to kill children," Irsu snapped. "We will not have this discussion again if it arises in the future."

"You're in command now?" Bordnu barked back at him.

"If you do otherwise, Mother will know."

Bordnu glared at him, then swiveled about to storm away.

The "threat of telling Mother" card had won. Neither son wanted to be the one to see her face broken in shame of her children. For his part, resorting to that tactic made Irsu feel like a suckling babe once more, but not in a good way.

He walked to the back door of the room, a kitchen, and kicked that door open. "These children are free to flee into the night," he yelled outward.

Then he stepped back and gestured at the kids, pointing to the door.

They didn't speak Dwarvish, but they understood that. Their backs disappeared into the darkness as quickly as spooked ponies, fortunately away from the slagged spitter nest.

He would kill humans. But he would not kill children of any kind. That was his line. And now it was Bordnu's line too, or Irsu would follow through on his threat.

Mother would not be pleased.

Chapter 13 - Detente

May 24, 1940

"We're not getting anywhere," Timothy yelled from behind the cab. "If we don't get moving, there won't be any chance to stay ahead of our new enemy because we'll be out of fuel."

Harry swung the door open and jumped out onto the roof of the Matador. It wasn't about to move anywhere, so the top was safe enough. Civilians and Allied soldiers swilled around the vehicle, clogging the roads south. At least they were no longer fleeing toward Dunkirk, where they'd be pushed into the sea. Now they were fleeing south from the horror of the dead rising near Arras.

Hans and Timothy leaned out of the lorry's bed to speak to Harry.

"We should go west from here, until we find clear roads," Hans said. "Then head south again."

"Into the German lines?" Timothy argued. "Are you crazy?"

"You think there are still lines?" Hans scoffed. "Are there British lines now? French lines? You think this isn't happening to the Germans?"

"Well, they are more deserv—"

"Shut it!" Harry barked. "This will get us nowhere. Hans, do you know there is a road west? We burn extra fuel going cross country, and the ground is wet from the storms. We risk being mired down."

"The storms!" Timothy said. "They're connected to these dead men somehow…"

"We don't know that, but it makes a lot of sense," Harry replied after a long pause. "We could head west, and if we stay in the dry zones maybe we won't encounter the dead."

Hans shook his head. "They can leave the rained on areas. It was dry just outside of your encampment to the south, the dead followed us when we left, no problem."

As if to accentuate his point, the crowd surged forward, movement coming from behind.

"Turn this thing off," Harry ordered Wilkes, leaning down over the roof of the cab to be heard.

With the engine dead, he could hear screams from the north, and panic was surging through the refugees like a concussion wave from a bomb.

He stood and raised his binoculars.

In the distance the skeletal soldiers of WWI marched south, in ranks much like they would have when going to war a quarter century earlier. The ranks broke as they surged against the tail end of the refugee line, and Harry watched in horror as the dead beasts took down the unfortunate souls at the rear of the exodus.

Men, women, and children… the monsters cut no quarter to any. As he scanned the horizon, he saw a continuous line of the creatures to the east as well.

"By the God above," he whispered.

"What is it?" Tim asked.

"We have to develop another plan," Harry responded. "Death isn't waiting for us to act, he's forcing our hand."

Harry helped Tim up on to the roof of the cab, which bowed a bit under the weight of the two men. He handed the glasses to his gunner's mate and friend.

"My God," Timothy spat out. "Barbarism!"

"Get in the bed. We need to go now," Harry said. "Before these civilians start to think we're their salvation and overwhelm us."

Timothy looked shocked but did as he was told. Harry swung himself off the roof, this time on the driver's side.

"Get over, Wilkes. I'm driving."

They couldn't go forward or backward, and to the east was more of the creatures. The west had Germans, but that was a better choice than the dead.

People were surging out into the fields, abandoning the road and the things they'd salvaged from their houses, or possibly stolen from the houses of others. Fortunately, most of Arras area had already evacuated before the dead rose from the ground, or the situation would be even worse.

Harry started the Matador, then drove it through a hedge into a field of early wheat. The heavy vehicle bogged slightly in the loosely plowed soil but didn't sink. He carefully worked the clutch and left the lorry in a higher gear so as not to spin the tires.

They bounced horribly as they ran perpendicular to the plow ruts, but they were getting away. People ran by, faster than the lorry could move on such horrid ground. A fact that probably kept the runners from leaping on the vehicle for safety and dooming them all.

When the situation couldn't get any worse, it did.

A dozen German tanks, Panzer IIs, burst through the hedgerow at the far side of the field.

"We're fookin' done for," Wilkes spat out, his voice angry.

"Language, Private Wilkes," Harry admonished. "Let's go out with dignity."

The civilians ran in all directions, but mainly away from Harry's team.

He stopped the Matador. They might as well die sitting comfortably instead of bouncing around like marbles in a sack.

To his surprise, the PzIIs turned south, followed by a few hundred German infantry on foot. Three much larger tanks, PzIVs from Harry's estimate although he'd never seen one, headed across the field toward his team.

The tanks stopped thirty meters distant, their guns at the ready. The top hatch of the right tank opened, and a German officer poked his head up.

"*Was ist deine mission?*"

"He wants to know your mission," Hans yelled around the cab.

"Tell him we're scouting the perimeter of this nightmare," Harry replied. "Trying to rescue any soldiers we might come across." It was as good of a lie as any, and technically, they were trying to save themselves.

Hans told his superior, and the officer identified himself as Lieutenant Colonel Karl Schmidt.

"*Wir haben den gleichen Feind jetzt. Kommen sie zu uns.*"

"He says we have the same enemy. Come with them."

Harry's eyes opened a bit wider. What a ridiculous offer, but he was in no condition to be impolite. "You can Hans, but I don't see me joining the Huns anytime soon. Even for what's going on now."

Rapid tank fire erupted from the south. The PzIIs were tearing into the line of the dead, parts of bodies flew everywhere. The dead men surged toward the new challenge, but for the moment the German tanks seemed up to the task.

Hans told the German something long and drawn out, which made the officer frown. Then a box was tossed out of the tank, onto the ground.

"*In der Nähe von Bapaume sind britische Truppen isoliert.*"

"British troops, he doesn't say how many, are isolated near a town east of here."

"What town?"

Hans asked the officer, but he didn't know more about it. He was sharing with them a report he'd been given, but not been part of.

"Thank him," Harry told his translator.

"Sehr gut. Wie werden sie."

"What did you tell him earlier when he threw out the box?" Harry asked.

"I told him my unit was destroyed. I'd like to work with you to save other soldiers, German, British, and French. I also asked for more ammunition for my Karabiner 98."

The Panzer IVs turned south to join their compatriots, opening fire with their machine guns. The near constant sound of gunfire made it hard to converse, so Harry jumped out and grabbed the box on the ground.

Ammunition, as expected. He tossed the box to Hans as he climbed back into the cab.

Maybe the Germans and the Allies could get along well enough to fight the invasion of the supernatural together.

"Wilkes," he yelled. "Take us west, to where it's quiet, so we can talk. The tanks will protect our flank from the dead men for long enough."

Wilkes nodded and started up across the field again, bouncing in the ruts. Hans sat back down hurriedly, after nearly being tossed out.

For some reason that made Harry laugh.

He was still grinning like a fool as the sound of battle lessened behind them, soon overwhelmed by the complaints of the Matador's groaning suspension as they beat their way across the field.

Once past the rough ground, Harry ordered Wilkes to stop. "Miller, break out the radio," he commanded. "Set it up, let's hear the situation."

Soon their most precious commodity other than ammunition was sitting on the lowered rear gate of the lorry, squealing as Private Miller rotated dials to draw in information from around the continent.

A French station passed by the dial, nobody in the unit spoke French.

A British station, probably from the Isles, wavered in and out on the edge of reception.

"Find something better," Harry ordered.

Soon a German station filled the speaker with rich sound, the spitting language practically drenching them from the wireless set.

"Translate, Hans."

"It looks like we've come in on the middle. The new Führer has announced a truce has been reached with the British, that all current front lines will be held in place until negotiations can be set up in Paris."

"Who's the new Führer?" Timothy asked.

"Herr Lutz Schwerin von Krosigk," Hans said.

"Who the hell is that?" one of the men asked, his contempt clear for all to hear.

"I have no idea," Hans answered, as if the question was sincere. "I have never heard of him."

"Well, if he wants to stop the fighting, then he's okay for now," Harry said. "We'll not fire on the Germans unless they fire on us, boys, we don't want to be the ones who take down the truce."

A mix of cheers and groans greeted his proclamation. He marveled at how soon the groaning men forgot the drubbing they were getting from the Germans just a week ago, when it was a valid question whether they'd spend their time in a prisoner of war camp or dead.

"That's the order," Harry demanded. "You'll like it, because I gave it."

"Shouldn't we be meeting up with the Expeditionary Forces near Paris?" someone else asked.

"We'll do so when we have orders to do so," Harry said. "Miller, see if you can raise an allied HQ. Tell them I'd like to look for our men behind German lines. Ask nicely."

"Will do," Miller replied.

They waited several hours for an answer, long enough for the Germans to finish their fight with the dead of WWI and move on. The dead would return to the area, that much was certain. They seemed to spread out as if they didn't want to be that close to each other. Unless the living was around, then they bunched up. Harry set up a guard perimeter to make sure they weren't ambushed as dusk fell.

Half an hour passed, and Miller didn't get a response.

"We should find a house, Harry, and wait for orders to come in. Maybe find some food in an abandoned building," Timothy told him.

"Stellar." Harry waved at the men to get in the lorry. "Pack it up, Miller. Wilkes, you're driving. There's a hamlet to the southeast, take us there. We'll find a barn to sleep in at the very least."

Thirty minutes after that they'd selected a two-story house, abandoned by the owners. After ransacking anything that remained in the kitchen, they occupied the second story for security and moved furniture on the first floor to block easy access up the stairs

They lit a fire in the second-floor fireplace and set up a watch. A third would watch three hours, then another third the next three, then the last third the last three. They'd all get six hours sleep if things went as planned.

In war, nothing goes as planned. It was after midnight when the first sign of trouble started. The fire had burned low, but it still cast out enough light to throw shadows on the walls. The watch team had an oil lamp that they could quickly light.

They lit it after hearing glass breaking on the first floor.

Four men guarded the top of the stairwell while the other woke the rest of the unit.

"So much for six hours," Timothy complained.

The sound of wood shattering came not much after, and soon the men were firing into the stairwell. Harry ran to see what was going on. The dead were trying to get past the dresser and couch they'd used to block the stairwell. Both pieces of furniture were severely damaged by the raw strength of the dead and by the rain of bullets.

"Be careful, take aim, hit them in the head," Hans advised. "We can't waste ammo, and only a head shot kills them."

"How do you know?"

"Because I killed one."

"I saw it," Wilkes confirmed. "Hans shot it through the head, just like he said."

Harry nodded. "You heard him. Take it slow. Two of us will fire from the top of the stairs, no more. After your MAS is empty, you step aside, and the next man moves in. Reload and go to the back of the line. Miller, you and Jenkins will be checking to see if any have climbed to a window trying to get in."

Miller grabbed Harry by the arm as he moved to pass the radioman in the hallway.

His voice sounded as if he were on edge. "What town is this, Sergeant? Did you see a sign coming in?"

"Bapaume," Harry replied.

Miller's face fell. "My father fought here in WWI. The Second Battle of Bapaume." He grabbed Harry's arm again and led him to a corner before speaking again in whispers. "At least twenty thousand died here, Harry. On both sides."

It was Harry's turn to be aghast. Arras wasn't the only battlefield. Battles were fought all over northern France. Harry and his men were traversing a nation sized minefield of the dead. And they were in the middle of the threat.

With a sinking heart he went to check on the men fighting at the stairs, and to see if they were holding up. If they started firing erratically, all would be lost. Effective ammo usage was their only hope as much of their spare ammo was in the lorry.

He'd told them the right way to conserve what they had. It was an efficient system. The dead were terribly frightening as enemies, but not smart at all. How they'd known to attack this house was speculation, but maybe it was the smoke from the fire. Maybe it was light flickering in the windows. Or maybe they could sense the living.

Harry walked back into the room where Miller was and looked out the window.

Hundreds, maybe thousands of dead circled the house. The ones nearby looked up at him with their half-formed faces, then reached to try to drag him down toward them despite being a dozen feet away. His heart sank further, as he pulled the curtains closed. "Miller, if you hear something at the window, yell. Otherwise keep working on that wireless. Get us some news."

"On it, Sergeant. If we had a larger aerial, that would help. But I'll make do."

Harry threw the mattress off the bed and propped the metal spring base up against the wall. "Hooking into that help any?" he asked.

"Genius," Miller said as he ran a wire to the spring set. "I'll be able to set up a directional antenna with that idea, I believe. Thanks, Sergeant."

It wouldn't do much good, Harry knew. Even if they used their bullets perfectly, there probably wouldn't be enough.

Then it would be bayonets, for those that had them. That might be good for one more kill, before a man was brought down by the clawing bones.

At least the dead weren't climbing on each other to get to the upper story windows. It was as if they were queuing up to see a movie, each waiting somewhat patiently for their turn to enter the house and take a bullet in the head.

Behind him he heard a trigger pull release a firing pin to click on an empty chamber. Someone yelled at the man with the empty gun to get the hell out of the way. The soldiers were stressed, but who wouldn't be? He couldn't tell who was screaming, the panic distorted their voice too much.

He got up to return to the stairwell so he could raise morale and restore order.

Hopefully his own morale would hold out, because it was going to be a long night.

He looked down at his pistol and resolved to save the bullets in it, and his reload, for the team. And one for himself.

Chapter 14 - Trapped

May 25, 1940

Surprisingly there was no issue with the amount of ammo Harry's squad had, because the dead clogged up the stairwell to the point they couldn't get past. As their re-stilled corpses fell to the incline of the stairs, the next attackers in line weren't smart enough to remove the bodies that fell in front of them, but merely tried to climb over.

Soon, with an accurate shot from the soldiers, that next attacker fell on the remains of those who came before, building a wall of bones and the shredded cloth of Great War uniforms.

Once the wall of gore was built, the dead didn't seem to notice the living among Harry's squad at all, unless someone made a noise. Then there'd be dissonant concert of whistling airways and grunts on the first floor, until his men were quiet for a few minutes.

Then they'd be forgotten. That meant they couldn't just feel the presence of the living. Something had to key them to it and keep their attention. Valuable information.

Harry tiptoed into the bedroom-become-radio-room to tell Miller to turn the wireless to the minimum volume.

As he approached the doorway, he noticed a strange reddish light illuminating the walls he could see within.

Another terror was something he wasn't sure he could deal with right now. Cautiously he peeked around the door frame, and his mouth fell open.

Miller was sitting on a chair, with his hand out before him, palm up. An orange light danced in the radioman's hands, bobbing up and down, turning in on itself like a fire with no place to go.

"Miller," Harry whispered. "What is that? Get rid of it."

The private looked up at him with awe. "I made this, Sergeant."

Harry braced his arms against the cold in the room. How did it get so cold? It wasn't that cold outside. Miller didn't seem to notice. "You made it? Have you gone balmy?"

"It was getting dark, I wished I had an electric torch so I could see to tune the squelch. Some sort of feeling I had inside me told me to extend my arm out, and when I did this appeared."

"How bloody long have you been holding that thing?"

"Twenty minutes," Miller said like he was reporting how long it had taken him to walk to the market.

"Can you get rid of it?"

Miller turned his hand over and the little fire winked out, and with it Miller's quiet attitude about the entire thing.

"I made fire!" he exclaimed.

The chorus of death that erupted from below made Harry slap his forehead. Hopefully the barrier his men had nervously named the Bone Barricade would hold.

Harry grabbed Miller's arm and shook him as he whispered a sharp admonition. "Shut your damned mouth, you." He let go of the man and walked to the window, looking out on the mass of dead men. "You'll get us all killed. We have to be as silent as possible When we are they forget we're here."

"I'm sorry, Sergeant," Miller whispered contritely.

"You were distracted," Harry admitted. "I've never seen anything like what you did there."

"Great for parties, I'd imagine," Miller whispered back. "Or when the batteries on the torch give out."

"Is it fire?"

"I think so," Miller replied. "I wasn't going to stick my other hand in it, but it warmed me."

"Made the rest of the room like an ice box," Harry said, still chilled. "Wonder if that's where it gets the energy? You weren't burning wood."

"Maybe. If we get out of here, I'll have to experiment."

"That you will," Harry agreed. "But it's *when*, not *if*."

"Of course," Miller nodded.

"Get some sleep, you've already done your watch. No need to spend tomorrow in a daze."

"I doubt I can, but I'll try."

"Good lad." Harry walked out of the room as Miller lay down on the mattress he'd pulled to the floor earlier for the aerial.

"What was his thing?" Timothy whispered.

"We'll discuss it tomorrow," Harry said. "One problem at a time is all I want right now."

It was hard to see Tim in the dark, but Harry thought the man shook his head. He clasped his friend's shoulder. "We're going to get out of this. Whatever it takes."

"You're in charge, Harry. It'll be a cold day in Morocco before you go down without a fight."

Harry didn't respond. There was no reason to fight and expect victory. If the dead didn't move on of their own volition, his men would starve, or die trying to break through the masses of skeletons and horror to safety.

At least this chalet had running water. Death wouldn't be because of thirst. The one bit of surprising good luck considering they were in a country where running water wasn't that common.

He'd be awake the rest of the dark hours trying to figure out a plan. They might stay one more day. After that, without food, they'd only grow weaker.

But better to die fighting than starving.

Chapter 15 - Stormfront

The storms of this world were no different than on Aerth. Lightning crashed, thunder rolled.

So did Iron Company. They rolled southeast, pass the direct effect of the gate. More than once the dwarves had skirted graveyards that writhed with the struggles of the dead.

Human dead.

That was why it was good to be dwarven. Dwarves did not come back to life to kill their own. Or others, for that matter. When a dwarf died, he had the dignity to remain dead, as it should be.

Humans, on the other hand, were even worse than the elves. The elves were bad enough, with certainty, but by Irsu's estimation it seemed like every human that hadn't completely turned to dust was trying to rejoin the living.

Judging by the screams coming from some of the houses near graveyards, a few of the undead were successful at the coming back part. If the teachings of the Ekesstu priests were accurate, as the dead killed more of the living, they'd grow stronger until their minds returned. Or at least some of their mind, because they'd have no shame for what they'd done to the living. No. The dead would see the living as sustenance and want more.

Dwarves were lucky in that sense too. The dead would seek out their own kind, for some reason. Maybe the dwarven souls tasted wrong. Or maybe dwarfs were the soulless bastards the elves claimed all along.

Irsu chuckled.

"What's the joke?" Coragg asked.

"Nothing, my friend," he answered. "Just reflecting on how these storms were no different than in the Iron Mountains. Loud, wet, and hard on the armor."

"We're going to need to source some leather," Coragg said, "since you mention it. The joints of these plate monstrosities will only last so long."

"Aye. Next field of cows, we'll harvest some."

They walked in silence for a while. The rain didn't let up, and the darkness it brought made traversing the fallow fields they were on harder. He'd hear a soldier grunt as a root grabbed his boot far more often than he would have thought possible for the warriors of Iron Company.

They were tired. They'd marched twenty hours a day for a long many days.

"Not many of the gray soldiers around," Coragg said. "I'm surprised they didn't come after us with you letting the children go."

Irsu growled deep in his throat. "Don't question that, unless you want a dent in that faceplate of yours."

"No, not questioning," Coragg replied. "Just saying I expected the kids to put the grays on our tail."

"I think one of those men was the father," Irsu said. "They probably have no joy left in their days to power their words. Grief will keep them silent."

"Maybe."

Rain spilled down through the minuscule gap between the visor and his helm. Several times a minute a drop would run down his nose, then drip into his beard.

"The dwarf in my squad I see killin' kids, I execute," Irsu said. "The one that murders children will murder anyone."

"We all know," Coragg confirmed. "You made that clear. I just have one question."

"Spit it out," Irsu grunted. "You deserve my thoughts."

"How are we supposed to do the Underking's bidding and take this world if we never deal with the children of the humans?"

"We're not going to kill the humans," Irsu said. "We're going to push them back through to Aerth. That's what Hagirr wants anyway. He wants his people back with him, and we want a world with almost no magic."

"So we're trading?"

"Best we can. Some are going to die," Irsu admitted. "But not the kids."

"Not the kids," Coragg agreed.

"Not the kids," several of the dwarves right behind them repeated.

Irsu laughed. He wasn't worried about his own troops. But for the first time he found himself wishing he was in charge of the entire company. Because his soldiers would obey. The others had different masters.

"Keep them in order," Irsu said. "I am going to talk to Bordnu."

"As you command," Coragg answered. "On me, you lumps!"

Lightning crashed nearby as Irsu stepped to the side of the marching column. As usual, his platoon was in the front. Bordnu's in the rear, ostensibly to guard the provision wagons.

As the lines of silver metal clad dwarves marched past, several raised their weapons in salute.

Irsu nodded at them. Dwarven soldiers outside his own platoon respected him. He should, if it ever came to it, not have trouble spreading his ideas.

But it would be better if Bordnu set the standards.

Finally, the front of Iron platoon came into view. Bordnu handed command over to his second and broke ranks to walk with Irsu.

"Why are you back with me?" his brother asked.

Irsu could tell Bordnu was still angry about the events at the house. Nothing had come of it, and no shame stained their blades. There should be gratitude for that, but instead there were thin lips pressed tight in displeasure.

"I want you to set our policy," Irsu replied.

Bordnu didn't say anything for a few dozen steps. Then he answered with a simple, "I have."

"No kids, brother." Irsu clasped Bordnu's shoulder. "We don't kill children."

"Is this because you think none of the daughters of our hearth will have children with you?" Bordnu asked. "Do you have some soft spot for wolf cubs too? Or maybe you might adopt an ogre child as your own?"

Red immediately welled up in Irsu's eyes. Clearly his brother was angry. But he would quickly make Irsu just as enraged if mockery was the path of conversation he would follow.

"We dwarves honor children of our hearths. We protect them, we coddle them, we raise and educate them. When a mate sees me as having what she wants for her future, I will find a wife, and I will father a brood like hasn't been seen in centuries. But I am just starting," Irsu replied, "and I do *not* think children carry the evil of their parents. Do not pick this fight with me."

"You shouldn't even be here," Bordnu grumbled. "Secondborn who haven't contributed to our numbers are supposed to see to that first, not seek out adventure."

"Don't you think I know that? The Underking asked me. What he saw in me I don't know, but I am not bragging when I say I wield this axe as well as you have ever wielded any weapon."

Bordnu didn't respond to that provocation. "If we both die, only my bastard daughter will carry the name, and then only until she is betrothed," he complained. "You, little brother, should be home, making sons with a round female."

"You have a daughter? Why have I not met her?"

"Did you hear the bastard part?" Bordnu asked. "I was indiscreet in my youth."

"Crackstone is a lousy name anyway," Irsu said. "She'll be better off marrying out of it. Maybe that is why I haven't found a partner. I mean, seriously, who wants a cracked stone?"

"Worthy or not, we are the only that carry it. Father was no warrior, he was a second son and a blacksmith. But when called to fight, he fought. Because he had us boys already. Irsu Crackstone," Bordnu pushed his shoulder, "needs to be home, bouncing a baby boy on his lap. Then, when the lad reaches an age to carry on our hearth, you can go to war."

"I need to be here, keeping you from disgracing your axe with the blood of children."

Bordnu stopped, grabbing Irsu's armor at the elbow, jerking him to a stop as well. His brother lifted his faceplate, so Irsu lifted his.

"If our family doesn't get to continue, why do you care about the humans?" Bordnu's volume rose over the length of the question.

Irsu was shocked by the fact the question even had to be asked. His family wasn't in competition with human lineage.

"Why?" his brother yelled.

"You did not seem to care so much about killing the humans when we were coming through the gate," Irsu said as the last of the Iron platoon soldiers passed them. "Why the change?"

"We came through the gate with a hundred and sixty-eight of us. We are already under a hundred and forty. Your platoon has taken a particularly hard hit in regard to numbers."

"And yet here I am," Irsu said.

"We will take no chances," Bordnu said. "No survivors from now on, as I commanded at the farm house."

"No," Irsu said. "This isn't right."

"It's my command," his brother sneered. "And you will follow it."

The Iron Mountain clan of dwarves worshipped four gods of the elements, each with two faces, one of each gender. A face of light, and one of darkness.

Mordain, Lord of the Air, of weather, also bore the face of the great female sky that brings panic.

Ekesstu, Mother of the Aerth, of soil, fertility, and a male face of death and rot.

Semesku, Purveyor of Fire, of warmth, but also of the male aspect of war and rage.

Zein, Master of Water, of rivers, but also of the angry feminine face of cold, ice, and erosion.

The gods mated, producing the things that dwelled between their domains. Mordain, for example, would mate with the feminine aspect of Zein to create rain. If Zein's aspect was strongest in the mating, storms would follow, or freezing rain, or flooding. If Mordain's was strongest, gentle rains would fall and nourish crops.

Lightning was such a mating between Mordain and Zein, although some clerics said it was Semesku and Zein. Whichever gods made lightning, it was hard to tell if the good or the bad was dominant in most cases, as the flash was over so quickly.

Such a flash struck down from above, lancing through Bordnu's helmet, killing him instantly.

Irsu watched as his brother's eyes lit from the inside, and then instantly rolled back in his head. Red hot slag spewed from his armor in several places as the burning lance of skyborne energy ripped through the metal to race into the ground.

His brother fell backward into the loose mud with a plop.

Irsu, but one step distant, felt nothing from the lightning bolt. But he felt everything from the death.

He threw himself on top of his brother's partially burned body, weeping with an agony only the loss of a brother could create. Smoke rolled out through the joints in Bordnu's armor.

To make it worse, his brother hadn't died in battle. He'd died at the hands of avaricious gods, or maybe at the hands of stupid bad luck.

No death for a warrior.

Irsu had no idea how long he wept over his brother, the cold rain on his back, drenching his body, didn't keep the time. It just reminded him that he wasn't dead as well.

After an unknown time Coragg knelt in front of him.

"We have a duty," Coragg said. "The platoon leaders have spoken. You're the leader now."

Was this his fault? Had his despair at Bordnu's order summoned the wrath of Zein? He'd wished to command the company, after all.

Irsu stood, then looked at the dwarves of Iron platoon. He set aside his agony and loss, then rose to the duty that stood like a road to follow in front of him. There would be time to question his role later. For now, duty called.

"Get his body into the wagons. We'll burn it when we find a dry place to do so."

"Do we make camp?" Coragg asked.

"Here? Exposed?" Irsu asked, a bit surprised Coragg would think him not strong enough to continue. "It might be a day dark with clouds, but it's not over. We march until it is."

"Shall I switch our platoon position with Iron platoon?"

"Them in front you mean," Irsu said, his voice trailing off. He thought about it for a minute as the sky continued to hammer his company. It was customary for the commanding platoon to guard the supplies in the fourth rank. If Irsu was one thing, it wasn't customary.

"No. We are Hearthfire, and I am Iron Commander Irsu Crackstone. We, Guard Commander Coragg Bloodgem, you and I, we lead from the front."

Coragg leaned in close to Irsu's helmet. He looked down at Bordnu's body before he spoke, as if considering the wisdom of his words. "You're an only son now. Your line—"

"Will end if the gods will it," Irsu said. "If they wish another to command this mission, so be it. I lead from the front."

"So be it," Coragg agreed. "I am your second. I serve your will."

"As you have since the day we met, my friend."

Irsu looked at the two Iron platoon soldiers gathering Bordnu's body, then reached down and picked up Bordnu's axe. "I'll see to this."

The two troops stared at him for a moment.

"Now!" Coragg bellowed. "In the wagon!"

They completed their task as fast as any dwarf could move.

Irsu marched to the front. He'd talk to the company later. The company had stopped marching with the death of Bordnu. That wasn't how dwarves covered ground.

They would keep moving. For now, they had to follow him into the storm.

He found solace in the sound of the synchronized steps of his soldiers, and of Coragg's voice as he led the column in song.

We are Iron, we march from our clan.
If we march agin you, the end is at hand.
But if we march for you, then upon you fate
smiles.
As the Iron marches in columns and files.

<the sound of metal axes hitting metal armor>

Our axes sharp, our wits the same.
War's not our life, it's just our game.
We strike and we fight, we crush and we win.
Then we march home, until fate calls again.

Some of the truest words Irsu had ever heard, sung or spoken. As he listened to the storm rage around them, he wondered if he should silence the troops to prevent the enemy from hearing them.

But then he realized this was not the time. Bordnu needed a sendoff, and Iron Company needed a morale boost even more as they faced uncertainty under a new commander.

The rain blew sideways, the lightning flashed, and whatever the reason, he knew the gods were hiding him from the gray warriors. His ancestors were watching. The gods were behind him. This moment was a defining crossroads in the history of the Iron Mountain clan.

Irsu, and his troops, would rise to that call.

They'd penetrate deeper into enemy territory, and, when the long march was done, reclaim a hold empty for ten thousand years.

Chapter 16 - Red Saviors

May 26, 1940

Harry awakened to a beam of sunlight creeping across his face.

He jumped up, remembering where he was, gasping as the recollection of where he was struck him in the chest.

The house was mostly quiet, except for the occasional creak of boards from the first floor as the dead walked around in their oblivious paths. Fortunately, he hadn't cried out as he awakened.

It was stupid to fall asleep. He was supposed to be on watch.

He crept down the narrow second floor hall of the chalet and peeked around the corner. Tim and one of the men guarded the stairwell, the situation unchanged.

Approaching and then kneeling next to Timothy, Harry's face glowed red with embarrassment. "I dozed off, Tim. I'm sorry."

"You needed it, mate," Tim answered. "You've been looking out for us since that mess in Roeselare started. We owed you a chance to recharge."

Harry nodded, grateful for his friend. "I'll double it tonight. You can sleep my watch and yours."

"Sort of defeats letting you sleep last night, doesn't it?" Tim whispered back to him in response. "Get over it. I did it for the men. They deserve a leader with a clear mind."

Smiling, Harry clasped his friend's back. "Anything from below?"

"Not a thing." Tim tapped his MAS. "The waiting is killing me. We can't leave, we can't stay, they're oblivious we're even here anymore. It's the strangest stalemate I've ever seen."

"It is," Harry agreed. "We won't act yet, but eventually we'll have to try to bust our way to the lorry."

"Death mission," Garrett, the private next to Tim said.

Harry shrugged. "So is starving." He stood back up and quit whispering. "We'll meet in the radio room inside the hour, I'll let everyone know. One person will guard the stair and miss the meeting, but I'll brief them separate."

"You have a plan?"

"We count our stores, bullets, grenades, food supplies, anything else that might get us to the Matador alive. We ransack this floor. Then we figure out where to set up the Hotchkiss, I'll cut an arc to the lorry with it."

"You'll be left here," Tim replied. "That's a bad plan."

"You could, once you get to the lorry, drive them down."

"One man can do that," Tim said. "We don't need to risk everyone else. One man makes it to the Matador, the rest cut the path."

"That's why I'm glad we're friends," Harry said. "Your idea is better. Bring the lorry to the house, we climb out the window on top, then you drive us off." He scratched his stubble covered chin. "That work?"

"Better than starving, but not much," Tim said. "I'll make the run for it. Someone must, and I'm not that great of a shot. Which is why you make me load the machine gun, don't deny it."

Harry laughed. "You win this one, Timothy Martin."

"Lucky me. Should rather win a poker pot."

Harry no longer cared to be quiet, the more of the things in the house, the fewer between the outer walls and the Matador. He clacked his boots against the floor as he walked toward the radio room. Groans and whistles greeted him from below. He called for the men to assemble with him and told them the plan.

"What stores do we have?" he asked the assembly. "Hans, you can hold back. Unless you have some grenades I don't know about."

The German shook his head no. "Can't hide those very well, big long sticks that they are."

As the men listed off their stores, it was apparent to Harry they needed to stock up better if they survived the day.

Six grenades, four cans of lighter fluid, for some reason Parker had a small can of black powder, and eight knives between the lot.

"Rightly pathetic," Harry said. "But for now, the grenades are important. Maybe the rest will come into play if we get desperate, but we already have no food up here, let's not add a fire to the problem."

"How do we deploy?" one soldier asked.

"Get a table in here for the Hotchkiss' firing position, and all the other windows on this side get two men each. Careful not the shoot the Matador, a flat tire or holed engine block and we're done."

"Why not knock some of the wall out to open up some more firing positions?" Miller asked.

"Smart one," Harry said, complimenting him. "You have a way?"

"Da is a miner back in Devon, pulling tungsten out of the ground," Miller said. They bore a hole, filled it with powder, then ignited it. Same would work for opening up a wall or two here."

"Can you do it?" Harry asked.

Miller smirked at him. The lad was confident, Harry had to give him that.

"Then get it on it. The rest of you take an hour to pick your spots and work out your fire zones. Decide who will wait for the wall to open to grab those spots. Miller, we open these walls for business at…" Harry looked at his watch. "Eleven AM."

Miller walked over to the wall and used his knife to start digging into the plaster to create a blast hole. "One of you get the radio out by the stairwell to keep it safe, and you clumsy oafs be careful with it. Parker, leave that powder, Wilkes, you leave your lighter fluid."

The men did as they were told, although Parker did so reluctantly. That made Harry wonder what Parker's particular psychosis was. Everyone had one, some were more dangerous than others.

"Can I help?" Harry asked Miller.

"Can you get some fabric and make a fuse, Sergeant?"

"How do I go about that?"

"Roll the powder up in the cloth like the lead in a pencil. Two heaping tablespoons per foot."

"You got it," Harry said, visualizing what Miller wanted. "I assume tight so there are no gaps?"

"You're made for this, Sergeant," Miller said, nodding his head as he dug at the wall. "That's how to do it."

An hour later they were ready, Miller had one hole finished with a lot of precision, in a second bedroom Wilkes had a similar, if less precise, hole. The wall was plaster, behind that the bricks the house was made of. Luckily, the bricks were brittle, and the mortar between them even more so.

"Hand me your fuse," Miller said.

Harry did so, alarmed to see Miller shake the powder out of three or four inches of one end. "I do that wrong?"

"Not at all. We want this end to burn slow so we can light it and get away. Once it gets to the powder, it will take off."

"Right. Makes sense." Harry would never have thought of that.

Once Miller had the fuse in the hole and the ends tied off with a bit of string to keep any more powder from getting out, he packed the hole with half of the remaining powder.

"That's a lot," Harry said. "You sure about this?"

"No, of course not. But it is a brick wall."

"Hard to disagree."

Once the hole was packed, Miller squirted a touch of lighter fluid on the end of the fuse that was cloth only. "It'll start without a delay," he explained.

They quickly packed the other blast hole; the process went even quicker.

"Hans, you take a lighter, you light that one," Harry said, pointing to Wilkes' room. "Miller, you light the one you dug. Everyone else to the stairs, know your positions after the blast, we're not going to waste any time. I'll be in the hall, counting down from three. At zero, you both light your fuse then bolt to the stairs."

It was a plan. How good of one was probably not something to be discussed, but what it lacked in sensibility it made up for in desperation.

"Three... two... one... now!" Harry yelled.

The men lit their fuses, which flared up immediately thanks to the lighter fluid. All three ran to the stairs, out of sight of the blasts. By the time Harry knelt and covered his ears he heard one of the black powder fuses catch.

An explosion rocked the house, two seconds later another did the same.

The troops uncovered their ears and raced to their positions. Two holes, each about three feet in diameter, greeted them for their efforts. The windows were all shattered and knocked out.

The men cheered. Something had gone right.

Harry heard something even over the groaning of the dead.

"Wait!" he barked as his men began pushing more bricks from the walls out onto the dead below.

Everyone stood silent.

"Is that a marching cadence?" Timothy asked.

"Get down," Harry hissed. "Everyone, get down behind cover!"

It was a marching cadence. But it wasn't in English, and it wasn't in German or French.

Harry peeked through a hole in the bricks and saw the dead rushing toward the new threat. At least two hundred of the short armored men were coming down the road, bellowing something in their guttural language that couldn't be anything else but a marching cadence.

Unlike the troops at Roeselare, these troops were wearing red armor. As he watched, the company commander of the enemy column ordered a stop.

He bellowed some orders and the otherworldly soldiers quickly formed three lines. The main barrier were soldiers with pikes with shields. They set themselves to receive the charge of the dead men. Kneeling in front of the pike bearers, ready to surge forward to dispatch any dead that passed the pike tips, were axes. Some of those had shields, some wielded two axes, some wielded axes so large both arms needed to carry them. Behind the pike soldiers, taking advantage of carefully maintained open space, were crossbowmen.

Harry had learned all too well to fear those.

The dead surged forward with surprising rapidity, making Harry wonder if Tim could have reached the Matador before the dead reached him.

"Should we open fire?" Tim asked, ready to service the Hotchkiss' hungry magazine breech.

"On which side?" Harry replied "No we'll let this unfold and deal with the remnants." He yelled loud enough to be heard from the other room. "Keep under cover, those crossbowmen will end you!"

The dead would ensure the battle would reach a defining conclusion for one side or the other.

Despite his own advice, Harry watched from a smaller hole below the main hole Miller blasted. The dead didn't disappoint his assessment of them. They assaulted the short men with fury, giving no quarter. The dead probably outnumbered the red company ten to one, but they didn't have the discipline the strange soldiers had. As a pike found a home in the body of one of the dead, a crossbowman shot it in the head while the pikeman tried to hold it still. Then the pikeman would jerk the tip of his weapon from the body, the dead would fall to make a barrier his fellows would have to deal with.

If for some reason the crossbowman couldn't fire, the axes ran forward to dispatch the impaled creature. Harry saw several of them dragged into the masses of the dead when they advanced too far. They disappeared under the mass of writhing skeletons and Harry shuddered at their fate, even if they were the enemy.

As the battle raged, the red company retreated strategically back up the road to keep room for their pikes to operate. Eventually, however, the pikes were overwhelmed, and the soldiers dropped them to the ground and drew short blades from scabbards at their sides.

"Arming swords," Miller said.

"What?" Timothy asked, incredulous.

"Arming swords. Those are close quarter weapons."

"How do you know this?"

"I like swords?" Miller replied. "Other kids played WWI when I was growing up. My friends and I played knights and … other knights."

"Didn't I tell you both to keep your heads down?" Harry snapped.

He was starting to develop a plan. Once the dead were gone up the road, he and the boys would have time to get out these windows and to the Matador. They'd race away from the short men and the dead men.

He waited until the time was right. Until the red company and the swarm around them was nearly a quarter mile up the road.

"Head for the lorry," he yelled. "We're making a break for it."

"There are still dead downstairs that didn't see the red guys," Tim said. "They'll hear us."

"Do you see a better opportunity coming?" Harry said, exasperated.

"No," Tim agreed as he pushed more bricks out onto the garden below.

"Guns at the ready, we're going out. Nobody is going to be left here, nobody is going to die here."

The squad seemed eager to take their chances.

"Tim, you go out, I'll lower the machine gun to you. Everyone get your gear, we're going now. Hans, Wilkes, get up on the back of the lorry and stand guard. Anything comes our way, open fire."

Less than a minute later everyone was on the ground. Nobody except the two appointed guards bolted for the lorry, and the guard team dispatched the first few outside dead that noticed them.

Harry's feet finally reached the ground where he grabbed the Hotchkiss he'd lowered.

"They're rising up inside the house," Tim said. "We need to go."

"To the Matador," Harry yelled, and ran with the gun. "Wilkes you drive. Follow the road away from the red company."

Thirty seconds after that the Matador rumbled to life and they were off once again, patting themselves on the back for their good fortunes.

Harry scanned the surrounding territory for enemies.

The dead walked everywhere he looked, their heads snapping toward the sound of the lorry as it passed by.

Their fortune would turn again soon, he knew.

Chapter 17 - What Border?

It was his twelfth day in this world, and for all purposes that mattered, it was *the* world.

His home was a distant and sometimes cloudy memory thanks to his exhaustion. His body was tired, his axe nicked, his armor dented from the spitter sticks the gray armies carried. During the march away from the gate his troops engaged the enemy six times, at a loss of twenty-seven soldiers. His brother in the mix made it twenty-eight.

At the moment they traveled down a good gravel road in an alpine area, dead on target for their destination if nothing stopped them.

His scout, the only one of the company not in iron armor, returned to brief him for tomorrow's march.

"There is a road block ahead, about a third of a full march," Scout Numo told him. "It's got dozens of the grays, but they're facing the other way. On the other side, twenty cart lengths beyond, there are other soldiers facing this way."

Irsu laughed. "You haven't traveled the underroads much, have you Numo?"

"I'm a surface scout, Commander."

"Where the Iron Mountain clan territory stops, we have the exact same setup with the subterranean areas around us. None shall surprise our hold."

"So, this is a border?"

"I should say it is," Irsu confirmed. "I wish we spoke the human languages so I could have you spy on them, or we had a priest here who could gift you with understanding."

The scout looked alarmed. "I didn't come here to have magic cast on me, Commander."

"Then you are fortunate that I don't have a priest with me."

Numo shook his head, unsettled that Irsu would force him to receive a spell. No matter, it was best the scout feared him a little. Fear enhanced job performance.

"Tell me about these soldiers on the other side of the border."

"Humans. Their uniforms are almost the same color, a bit more blue-gray I suppose. But they wear different insignia. No armor at all except the helmet, just like the grays. Humans seem to think their noggins are the only thing that matters."

"Was there hostility between the two sides?"

"Well, they did have a wall, and the road was barricaded with a lift gate, much like the surface road out of Iron Mountain where the caravans are inspected," Numo replied.

"I see." Irsu tugged at his armor to relieve himself of a section rubbing his skin. "Maybe they don't wear armor because it chafes."

"You should try leather, Commander. It's most liberating."

"I'm sure it is. The problem with wearing leather is everyone holds their money purse more tightly when you're near."

"Maybe."

Irsu gestured toward Coragg, who had his axe and shield both on the left arm. His right gripped his money pouch tightly, unaware that the scout and commander were talking about him.

Numo laughed. "Now that's funny."

"Coragg, we're breaking early," Irsu barked. "Stop the column, get the company off this road, and set up camp. Make sure our fires are shielded. Get that cow down off the provisions wagon. Roast it up."

"Something going on?"

"We're about to travel new territory, and tomorrow we're going to kill more humans. We're down to a hundred and thirty-six soldiers, I want them well fed and deprived of nothing when we do."

"Numo, how many humans guard the border?"

"Probably eighty of the grays. I only saw twenty or so of the others, but I didn't go to their side of the border. Razor wire and sturdy fencing in both directions from the road made passing over problematic other than at the road barricade."

"Good. Get some rest, tomorrow you'll scout numbers again before we attack."

"As you will," Numo said officially before disappearing into the trees.

"Where's he going?" Coragg asked. "He doesn't want some beer?"

"Who knows? Probably saw something he wants to explore, or steal."

They spent an hour setting up their camp, building banked firepits that would shield their light from onlookers who weren't up on the mountain sides. There wasn't anything to do about that, although this land seemed sparsely inhabited.

"We're close, Coragg. Another five or six days."

"You're bold to travel the roads. Twice we've nearly been seen by the humans riding in their machines."

"I wouldn't mind having one of those, would you?"

"One of those infernal devices?" Coragg scoffed. "No thanks. They even smell gnomish as they pass."

Behind them one of the soldiers skilled at butchering animals prepared the cow they'd absconded with earlier in the day. The farmer they took it from would probably attribute the loss to predation.

The butcher handed out multi-pound chunks to each fire circle, judging how far the meat would go. There were probably hundreds of pounds, certainly enough to feed the company tonight and maybe in the morning as well.

After the meal he talked about life back in Iron Mountain with Coragg, the other three soldiers sharing their fire listened intently. Since Irsu had taken over they'd eaten better and avoided conflict when they could. Most were grateful for that, they wanted to get home alive, not die heroes.

Still, in the morning they'd get enough wood and put it on the carts, so they could burn the bodies from tomorrow's battle. Dwarven only, since the human bodies seemed to want to get back up not too long after they were killed, and that would delay anyone who might be following Iron Company.

The dwarves deserved a proper sendoff. The wood was for them.

Irsu didn't have to stand watch, but one of the soldiers in his circle did. When he got up, Irsu asked him about it. "You go to sleep, I will stand your watch," he said after he figured out where the youngster was going.

"I—"

"Will kill more humans than me tomorrow because you'll be rested," Irsu interrupted. "What position is yours?"

"White two," the soldier replied. "Thank you, sir."

"I need time to think anyway."

Coragg laughed, looked at Irsu, then crawled toward the canvas tarp they shared as a tent. "Off with you then, you have guard duty."

Irsu shook his head and put on his chestplate and helmet. The pauldrons, gauntlets and greaves he left behind. Picking up his axe he considered snagging the ties for the tent Coragg was in, but then he'd need it to sleep in later.

The weather did look like it could rain again, as it had half their time on Earth so far. As uncomfortable as it was, the rain shielded them from view and may have been responsible for them getting this far. He didn't want to sleep in it without the waterproof canvas over his head, however.

The night passed slowly, he spent the time developing a plan based on the information Numo had given him. A border checkpoint would have useful information. Probably maps, books, maybe a translation guide if the people on each side of the border spoke different languages. With that if he gained knowledge of one language, he'd know how to understand both.

He'd order it all taken. They were close to their destination. The people who controlled the land they were passing into might be the ones who controlled the mountain they were seeking.

He returned to the fire ring to see Coragg up, cooking a hunk of meat.

"Eat," his second commanded.

Irsu took the meat and tore a bit off. "I'm grateful."

"Don't be. Cows are big. Meat is going to waste."

Irsu laughed. Of course, Coragg was practical, but he knew the gruff warrior cared as well.

"Why are you up?"

"To make sure you eat," Coragg replied. "And I can't sleep."

"Neither can we since you keep talking," someone said from a tent nearby.

Presently three warriors joined them and started roasting more meat. The smell was delightful.

"You know, it's a miracle if we're able to find this lost hold," Coragg said.

"What do you mean," Irsu asked. "We have clear directions."

"Last time our people marched here the ice was a thousand dwarves thick in many spaces. To the north of us ice ran all the way to the Great Northern Sea. Hairy elephants and great bears roamed the land. The humans didn't come to an easy place to live. They came to a hard place that has softened. The hard years made them tougher than the legends of them reveal. And made them clever as well."

"They barely provide any resistance," one of the soldiers said.

"Individually, maybe not," Coragg replied. "But nearly thirty of ours are dead, did you expect that from the humans?"

The soldiers shook their heads no.

"Soon that part of our test will be over," Irsu said. "And the next will begin."

"So it will."

"What comes next?" one of the soldiers asked. The other two punched his arm.

"No, it's alright, let him ask," Irsu said after he chewed a bite. "Next we find the mountain we are looking for. In the old days we named it Nollen, but that is not what the humans call it, I'm certain. When we find it, we find the ancient stones to let us inside."

"That doesn't sound so bad."

"When the time comes, you remember those words," Irsu said. "We will pay for our entrance in blood."

"Oh."

The troops ate the rest of their meal in silence then returned to their tents.

Coragg and Irsu did the same, no more words passed between them.

They instinctively felt that more hardship was coming. Irsu knew both he and Coragg could feel a trial was coming, but not what the trial was. Maybe it would be on the journey. Maybe it would be inside the hold itself. If there had ever been scrolls that contained the secrets of the Lost Hold, they'd decayed away ages ago with no surviving copies.

Irsu sighed. His worry would get him nowhere. Rest was the medicine he needed now.

Soon Coragg's snoring lulled Irsu into his own.

Chapter 18 - Behind All the Lines

May 27, 1940

A morning smoke is a delightful thing. The rush of nicotine into the lungs filled his soul with gratification. The health effects of cigarettes were well known to the Western world. A stimulant that cleared the mind and activated the body for a day of, well, in this case, war. (author note: *not true, see glossary*)

Harry flipped the spent smoke onto the ground.

Miller played with the radio, looking for any station still live that might provide any information. A group of French children stood around watching. One of them spoke broken English, so if Miller found a French station that was still broadcasting, Harry planned to put the kid to work.

For a smoke, probably.

His radioman had worked out a lot of details regarding their situation over the last two days. To the east a line of the dead stretched from the Maginot line down to south of Paris, in a death zone usually at least five miles wide. Trying to get through that line wasn't something Harry was willing to do, even if the reports were sporadic and mostly from the air. Heading west to join the main of the British Expeditionary forces was out of the question.

On a bright note, he'd been promoted. Headquarters determined that it was unsuitable for him to be a sergeant considering the task they had for him, so they promoted him to Lieutenant. His new rank wasn't reflected by his uniform, but that was the least of his worries.

HQ, still based at Dunkirk with the evacuation on hold, determined that Harry, having access to a radio and a working knowledge of the enemy, would reform and organize the British troops on the east side of what was now titled The Dead Zone.

Harry saw several problems with that. First, he had a very limited working knowledge of any enemy. He knew that to kill the dead they had to be shot in the head, which was the limit of his intel. Or maybe they could be stabbed. He wasn't sure. Secondly, he hadn't seen a living British soldier, or civilian for that matter, since the camp at Arras had been overrun and sacked by the risen soldiers of WWI. Many of which had probably been British, so there was that. The dead Brits didn't seem interested in being reformed or reorganized, other than at the biological level.

Thirdly, he was really only interested in avoiding contact with the Germans, the short men, or the dead until he could get far enough south to turn westward toward the coast. But if he had to, he'd go to the Mediterranean and steal a boat to get his men home.

He was, quite honestly, getting desperate.

Food stocks were what they could find in abandoned houses, but those supply sources were becoming less common as they moved south. A lot of French civilians simply didn't believe the story about the dead, even if Miller played it for them on the radio.

It was, Harry admitted, something that had to be seen with one's own eyes. It also annoyed him that old fat French men looked at him and his men as if they were cowards. And because of that, often deny the Brits any aid.

"I'm about to turn to robbery," Harry said to Timothy.

"Robbery?"

"Yes. In the days of the knights, Miller informed me, it was expected that friendly or enemy peasants would provide food for the nobility. Shelter and supplies too, if need be. Often such sustenance would simply be taken by force."

"We're the farthest things from nobles, Harry. You're a bloody sheep farmer, for Pete's sake."

"Nothing ignoble about that occupation," Harry replied indignantly.

"No, but you're not a nobleman. Those times are gone anyway."

"Do you like eating?" Harry asked.

"I do."

"Then we're taking a few of those chickens over there for our pots. Protocol be damned."

"Harry!"

His mind was set. He marched across the street to an occupied house, opened the gate to a picket fence, and walked into the garden.

He strode straight to the coop, then opened the door to drag out a few hens.

What happened next made lights flash behind his eyes. How he hadn't seen the woman he wasn't sure, maybe he was simply focused on the task of stealing, so alien it was to his character. But something struck him on the back of the head from behind, much to his surprise.

He turned around to see a young woman, probably in her mid-20s, glaring at him while holding a shovel.

She berated him in French. Or at least he assumed that's what she was doing.

"I can forgive you for hitting me, miss, but I'm taking a few of these chickens." He turned around to open the coop door again.

WHACK!

This time she took him to his knees, and then hit him again. Over on his side he went. She was yelling at him in a tone that wasn't friendly at all, and while he couldn't blame her, he had no idea what she was saying. His head hurt like she'd hit him with a shotgun.

He could still see, his men were laughing as they burst into the yard, intervening between his assailant and his body. She waved the shovel at Timothy, who approached her with his hands up.

Even the kids watching Miller came running over.

"Vous ne volerez pas mes poulets, ils sont tout ce qu'il me reste!" she yelled.

"She say you can not steal her chickens, she has nothing else," the translating boy spat out.

"Sounds like she's got your number, Harry," Timothy said. "We'll make it another day without if we have to."

Harry stood up, a bit wobbly. "Tell her we're sorry, we haven't eaten in a day or so, and she can't stay here anyway."

The kid told her.

"*Pourquoi je ne peux pas rester ici?*"

"Why can she not stay here?"

"The dead are coming," Harry said, his voice clearly indicating his desire not to fight the woman or her shovel.

"*Vous êtes l'homme fou qui parle des morts dont les vieux rient?*"

"That's me," Harry admitted after translation. "I'm the crazy guy all the old men are laughing at."

She spoke to the boy a moment, who then looked at Harry and wagged his finger. "No chicken, but you wait here."

The young woman ran inside and came out with a sack.

She handed it to Timothy, who thanked her.

"What is it?" Harry asked.

Tim looked in the bag. "Beets."

He hated beets. But this was no time to be picky.

"We'll be going ma'am, thank you." He looked at the boy. "Tell her I said that."

When they turned around, Timothy dropped the bag on the ground. The woman cursed, Harry assumed, then ran inside her house.

Thirty to forty of the red armored dwarves were in the street, staring at Harry's squad with their crossbows raised.

"*Ingrith don makul debrithi?*" one said, stepping forward. The talkative one had a gold braid on his shoulder plate, so probably a leader.

Harry stepped forward as well, toward the picket gate. "No idea what you're saying mate, but you got us dead to rights. I'd highly appreciate it if you didn't murder us."

Goldie listened as another short person, one dressed in a bath robe, spoke.

Bath Robe was wrapped in clothing much like a Moor woman. From head to toe. If Robes didn't have a beard, Harry would be sure it was Goldie's ball and chain.

Robes waved his fingers about and sang a little song.

"We have no intention of murdering anyone," Bath Robe said in perfect English after the song and finger dance.

Harry's hands fell to his sides in shock. He rushed toward the fence, causing the crossbow soldiers to raise their weapons as a precaution. Harry put his hands back up.

"You speak my language!" Harry said excitedly. "I didn't expect that."

"For the next several minutes at least," Robes confided. "After that I'll need a bit of time to speak to you again."

Harry wasn't going to ask what that was about. With all the strange happenings, Robes was probably using magic.

"If you're not here to kill our people, why are you here?" Harry asked.

"To send you through the gate," Robes said.

By the mannerism and voice, not to mention the projections on the front of Robe's clothing, Harry was starting to think he was speaking to a female after all. "Through the gate? That thing over Rotterdam? Not bloody likely."

"You'll go soon enough," she assured him, and he decided it was a she after all, "because it will be lonely when everyone you know goes to the other side and you are without a clan."

"What's on the other side?" Timothy asked from behind him.

"A world much like this one. Trust me, you belong there, not here," Robes said, sounding surprisingly friendly.

"And who then will be here?" Harry asked. "We like this place just fine."

"We won't make you go. But if you resist, eventually something much uglier than us will make you go. Or just kill you," Robes advised him.

"A threat?"

"A warning. There are many factions coming through to this world. Ours has a strict code of conduct that means we will not force you to go through. But we will ask. And warn you that if others find you, it may not be so polite of a meeting."

"We met your kind who wore black armor," Tim mentioned.

"Another clan. Black is the color of night, a warning. Mordain's evil is unleashed at night," Robes said.

"Mordain?" Harry asked. "Is that your leader?"

"One of our gods," Robes answered. "Knowing our gods will do you no good, they are on our side."

"Avoid black. Red is a fair lot. What other colors?" Harry asked.

"Silver is *entelgri makcht destimarkith gu nop*—" She stopped when the look on Harry's face changed to puzzlement. Whatever gave her the ability to understand him, it was over. She didn't know English after all.

Goldie ordered his men to take the chickens in the coop. One picked up the bag of beets and laughed at Timothy on the way past.

"Well dammit," Tim said. "I like beets."

Harry heard a few of the soldiers behind him grow restless and jingle their gear. "Let them go, boys, we're lucky to have our skins," he ordered.

The French woman came rushing out to stop the short men, but they pushed her aside. She lost her balance and the shovel flew loose from her hands.

The point of it struck Harry in the ribs, bringing tears of pain to his eyes.

"Bad luck, mate," Timothy said, comforting him.

As he recovered, Harry was embarrassed that he could do nothing to help the French woman.

Suddenly she and Harry were on the same team, the same side of this conflict. The side of humanity. This despite wishing to steal two of her chickens himself but moments before. At least he'd planned to just take two. The strangers took them all, probably twenty, wringing their necks and killing them on the spot. They took a dozen or more eggs as well.

Whoever the red company was, they weren't hostile, at least not overtly. But they were willing to leave the people here without food stocks. They stole all the chickens on the street, as well as a few cats and a goat as if it was something they were entitled to.

"That's what I'm talking about, Tim," Harry explained. "See how they just expected the food? We need to start just expecting the food."

"I guess you're right," Tim said.

The woman rushed back into her house, coming back out a few minutes later while Miller looked to see if the short men missed any of the eggs.

"Vous n'avez pas pris assez? C'est bien, vous allez me prendre au sud avec vous. Je n'ai plus rien, vous les sales Britanniques."

The kid translator spoke to them for her. "She say you are dirty British men, and she is wondering if you have taken enough from her. You will take her south, she has nothing here now."

Harry shrugged. "We didn't actually take anything from her," he responded, holding his head. His fingertips had traces of blood on them when he looked. She'd hit him but good.

She pursed her lips and walked over to the Matador, climbed up on the side rail and opened the door. She turned toward Harry as if he was remiss in not helping her inside.

Harry ran toward her. "Alright, you can come. But you have to ride in back."

"*Vous devez monter à l'arrière,*" the kid told her.

She huffed, stepped down from the cab, and walked around to the rear gate where she again waited for help up.

Sighing, Harry surrendered. Crazy times indeed. "Get her up there, boys, and hands off otherwise. We're British soldiers, we behave."

"Unless we're hungry," Wilkes said. "Then we steal chickens."

"Or just take a shovel upside the head," Timothy laughed.

"Drive," Harry ordered. "I'm still hungry, and not in the mood."

The rest of the soldiers, despite their grumbling stomachs, laughed. Harry could sense their relief at meeting an enemy that didn't just try to kill them on sight and might not be an enemy at all.

"Head east when you can, Wilkes. I don't care to see the red soldiers again. We'll head south tomorrow and find a place to drop our stowaway."

His stomach grumbled.

"Dammit, Wilkes. I wanted chicken soup."

Wilkes grinned. "Next town, Lieutenant." He gave Harry a thumbs up. "You can rob them blind for all I care."

Somehow it just sounded pathetic if someone else said the idea.

"We need a map," Harry said. "We have to stick to the abandoned areas if we're going to find food without looking like arses or fools."

"We can't drop our passenger off in an abandoned area," Tim said.

"If we have to, she can walk south," Harry said, uncomfortable with the idea. "But if we see refugees, she joins them."

"What do you think of that, Wilkes?" Timothy asked the driver.

Wilkes didn't answer, instead shifting the lorry up a gear. "We'll need diesel too."

"Abandoned towns," Harry reasserted. "That's the way."

Wilkes nodded.

Chapter 19 - On Top

May 27, 1940

Ernst and his team were on a prototype aircraft, a Henschel HS-130. This plane's first flight was a mere week before and it had performed well enough at altitude that it was selected to give Ernst's team a look at the gate over Rotterdam.

The aircraft was a slow climber, but it was perfect for what they needed. It had a service ceiling of over 12,500 meters and a range of over 2,500 kilometers. The payload was a camera package in what would normally be the bomb bay. They needed it to take pictures of the gate for later study.

An oxygen canister hung at Ernst's side, although the cabin was pressurized. As a prototype, nobody was entirely sure the HS-130 would even return to base with the cabin intact. Everybody kept a canister on them in case of a panel blowout and stood ready to connect to the pipe air supply if problems arose.

It was cold, causing Ernst to shiver in his chair. The control panel for the reconnaissance cameras was on a table, which normally would seat four controllers for the optics. For this mission there was only one, and Ernst sat at one of the open positions.

"It's all about Saint Lawrence Cathedral," Ernst told the cameraman. "If you get nothing else, get that image."

"I will try, Herr Haufmann."

"You will succeed, or I will give you a look up close and personal. Without a parachute," Ernst threatened.

"But we must develop the film to know, I can't do that here."

"Then if you fail I will find a different fate for you."

The man responded to the threat with silence, which Ernst decided was a sign of understanding. The stakes were very high for this mission. He clicked his earmuffs over to the pilot's channel.

"—*assieren 8.000 meter*," one of the men up front said.

8,000 meters. Good. Ernst knew what the dragons could do. He didn't know what their limits were. The higher the plane went, the safer he felt. Either the dragons wouldn't see them at such a distance upward, or the dragons wouldn't be able to climb so high.

If one of those things didn't save them, then this trip would be short and his pretend suicide a week ago would have been better if it had been real.

He keyed his microphone, still on the pilots' channel. "How long until we're over Rotterdam?"

"Thirty minutes, Herr Haufmann," one of them replied.

"Good. Advise me ten minutes out. I wish to see this with my own eyes."

"Heil, von Krosigk!" the man said as an answer.

"Heil, von Krosigk," Ernst answered dully. The Third Reich's Finance Minister was now the Führer. How droll. As if funding wasn't already tight enough.

Ernst closed his eyes and studied the drone of the aircraft's massive twin engines while it struggled higher.

"*Wir passieren 9.000 Meter,*" the pilot said, rousing him from his reverie.

"Dragon!" someone shouted on the channel. "Six o'clock low, beating his wings to catch us."

Ernst unstrapped himself from his chair, then made his way aft. He passed the camera package to see a man lying on the floor of the fuselage, looking out a window facing downward. He tapped the fellow on the shoulder.

The man rolled partially on his side and uncovered an ear.

"Are you the one reporting a dragon?" Ernst yelled at him.

"Yah," the fellow confirmed. "Down below, some distance away. Closing fast."

"Let me see," Ernst commanded, and the man slid to the side to share the viewport.

It took Ernst some time to find the creature, it was so distant. The man was good.

"How far away is it?" Ernst asked.

"Five kilometers is my guess, but I don't know. It depends on the size."

Ernst stared. This dragon was red, which should have made it easier to find, but didn't. He stared at it, pondering if this was the end.

An unsettling fear gripped his stomach. That wasn't normal. He wasn't one to cringe.

He steeled himself and looked out the window again. It was gaining on them.

"How far below us?" he asked the man.

"A thousand meters," his viewing companion answered.

As time passed the dragon was clearly not on an intercept course. It was catching them over the ground but would probably not be at their altitude when it did.

"Do you know how high we are?" Ernst demanded.

The man looked to his side, where a small bank of gauges stared back at him. "In a few seconds, 10,000 meters."

Maybe the creature did have a maximum altitude?

Two minutes later it was directly below them, probably eight hundred meters distant according to his viewing companion.

Its head turned to the side and it glared upward at the aircraft. Ernst felt fear in the pit of his stomach again, and the man beside him yelped.

"Tell the pilots not to look down under any circumstances," Ernst ordered the man. "Have them climb as fast as possible."

The dragon rolled over on its back and its neck lanced upward toward their flight. The belly of the beast glowed orange, which quickly rose up the neck plates. The mouth opened, and fire shot toward them in an ever expanding wall of flame.

Ernst screeched in unison with his companion.

The heat of the flame caressed his face, but the flames didn't reach the HS-130. They faded out into black smoke a few hundred meters below, then the smoke rapidly disappeared behind the plane. As they moved past the blackish haze, the dragon was below them and plummeting toward the ground.

So, the altitude limit of that dragon was near 10,000 meters. Was that true for them all?

He'd have to recommend that be tested. Quite a few German aircraft could reach that altitude. Even the fighters, the Bf-109s, would be able to climb above the reach of the dragons if this one dragon's limitations reflected them all.

Ernst grinned. He may have just found a critical weakness in their new enemy, one only the Germans would know about. If they could take down some dragons from above, maybe the creatures would learn it was best to attack toward France and Britain, not east toward a dangerous enemy like the Germans.

He'd learned the first useful thing of the day.

"Seven minutes to target," the speaker nearest him called out. He must have missed the ten minute warning in the chaos of the dragon attack.

He rushed forward to the cockpit. Visibility was excellent from the nose viewport, and he planned on sitting in there for the flyover.

"Six minutes," the pilot said.

Ernst settled into his observation spot with binoculars.

The ground below didn't look like Belgium. It was a semi-arid terrain, with sparse bushes and clumped grasses.

"Pilot, this terrain isn't correct," Ernst observed. "Where are we?"

"We are on course," the pilot replied, irritation in his voice. "The navigator is good."

The aircraft lurched.

"Something isn't right," the pilot said to his co-pilot, forgetting his channel was open.

"The compass is spinning wildly," the other responded.

"Your microphones are open," Ernst pointed out. "Idiots."

They silenced their conversation, which infuriated Ernst. Angry, he jumped up and pushed into the cockpit. "The terrain is wrong. I think we are over the world the dragons come from."

"We are flying the plane," the pilot snapped at him.

Ernst stomped back down to the observation deck. Below him something was happening. Lifting his binoculars, he saw a great stone arch running from one point on the ground to another. Wagons and what looked like soldiers streamed through it, disappearing from his view. A dragon sat on the ground nearby, next to a small tower of some kind.

"We are on the other side!" Ernst yelled. "We have passed through the gate!" He keyed up, barking orders at the cameraman. "Get filming if you're not."

Ahead of them, to the west, a strange phenomenon arced across the sky. Streaks of energy played along a curved plane, flashing in waves along a clearly defined barrier between Earth and the other world. The sky was clear above them, but ahead, past the energy field, storms flashed in squall lines over what looked like water.

Was that the English Channel?

"What is the weather along the Channel?" Ernst asked the pilot.

"Please Herr Haufmann, we—"

"THE WEATHER. NOW!"

"Storms, squalls from over the North Sea heading south. Cool weather, below seasonal averages."

He played his binoculars along the storm clouds. Those were definitely over water.

"Take us lower, we need to measure the width of the energy field."

"What are you talking about?" the pilot asked.

"TAKE US LOWER!"

The plane banked and started to spiral downward. Ernst, with no data to back up his risk, felt that over the gate he'd be safe from the dragons.

He spoke to everyone on the plane. "Does anyone see the city of Rotterdam? The cathedral?"

No answers.

He moved his observations to look in different directions as the plane spun in lazy circles. As they descended he could see more clearly into the other world.

To the north past the gate lay a chain of mountains, snowcapped and rugged. Much like the Alps, maybe taller. It reminded him of his visit to Nepal, as unpleasant as that was.

To the east was a continuation of that mountain chain, only closer. The peaks showed little weathering, the chain was young.

The south presented a dry landscape, with green streaks along rivers that flowed further south from his vantage point.

To the west the overlapping world revealed a desert, one which would make the Sahara proud. He saw sand dunes disappearing into the distance, with rocky buttes jutting from among the waves of sand.

Something caught his eye.

North of the arch a blimp floated serenely over a mass of individuals below. The blimp was short and bloated, unlike the streamlined zeppelins of the German air service.

He zoomed in as far as the binoculars would let him. It was hard to see with the jolting of his aircraft, but it looked like the blimp was powered by a coal fired boiler. Black smoke stretched out behind the craft, and a large single propeller pushed it in what seemed to be a circle over the creatures beneath it.

Either the lift didn't come from hydrogen, or these people were idiots using an open flame boiler. Ernst didn't believe an idiotic people would survive long enough to conquer the sky, they'd be smashed by an enemy long before that.

Those creatures on the ground, were they all coming through the gate?

"Are you getting pictures?" Ernst demanded of the cameraman.

"Thousands, Herr Haufmann."

"Excellent. Keep taking them until we are back over Germany."

The plane spent fifteen minutes spiraling downward, until Ernst could see the area around the arch quite well.

Were those German troops by the archway? They looked like prisoners, with men in metal armor guarding them. A wagon pulled by elephants, loaded with some of the prisoners, was heading away to the north.

The dragon seemed indifferent to the aircraft. It was now laid out on the ground, asleep as far as Ernst could tell. On the tower two men stood. One in a gray uniform, potentially a German soldier, the other in a blue bath robe or night gown.

"Get pictures of that tower. Lots of them," Ernst ordered.

The fellow with the robe started dancing.

"What in the world?" he whispered.

A blue bolt of energy shot from the man's outstretched hands and raced upward toward them.

"Incoming!" Ernst screamed. "Climb! Climb!"

The pilot swung the plane wildly back to the east, obscuring Ernst's view of the tower. The turn didn't block Ernst's view of the effect the bolt of energy had, however. It shot upward from under the aircraft, slamming through the port side wing. Metal rained upward and then backward. A large hole, half a meter across, was torn through the airfoil. For a moment white smoke poured out, but then stopped.

"South! Away from that tower!" he screamed into the mic.

No more attacks came, but the plane felt sluggish. It felt like the pilot was struggling to keep it from turning left as he climbed southward.

"When you get to 10,000 meters," Ernst said, "head home. This mission has been wildly successful."

The pilots didn't answer him.

Maybe they were working too hard to keep the plane under control with the damage. But he knew they'd heard. Everyone heard Ernst, that's just how life worked.

Chapter 20 - Toward Nolen

The conquest of the border barricade had gone well. The Iron Company secured maps, some of the spitter sticks, and rations. Strange rations, wrapped in metal plate. Weird that the humans armored their food but not themselves.

Attacking the grays on the north side of the border had been simple, the Iron Company butchered those humans without a loss. The Blue-Grays, as his soldiers were now calling the troops from the south, didn't help the grays at all. They simply watched as the north squad died.

When the Hearthstone platoon pushed up against the barricade with intention of passing through toward Nollen, the blue-grays became animated. Their leader and Irsu argued for a good while, neither understanding anything about the other or any words spoken, except that the Iron Company wanted to pass, and the enemy didn't want them to.

It could be an impasse, but that wasn't the plan. After tiring of hearing what he assumed was no in the strange human language, he slammed down his face shield and stabbed the soldier in front of him through the throat with the spike on the end of his axe shaft.

The rest of the enemy immediately attacked with their spitter sticks, but by then the crossbows were reloaded from killing the first set of soldiers.

It was a slaughter. Forty or more of the humans went down immediately. Inside of two minutes the remaining twenty or so succumbed to the pikes and axes.

Two of Irsu's soldiers suffered wounds, two more were dead.

"Put ours in the cart. You two wounded, ride there as well. We will tend to your needs when we get to the Lost Hold," Irsu ordered.

Coragg yelled in his patronly way toward the company, and soon they were all once again in columns. None too soon, the grays were already beginning to twitch as whatever was bringing back the humans from the dead seeped into their corpses.

"Double time," Irsu ordered. "For a dozen kadros. Then we return to normal pace."

They ran for fifteen minutes or so, then returned to a normal pace to regain their strength and their ability to fight if need be. The formation was also a lot louder when they ran, something Irsu wished to avoid.

"Do you hear that?" Coragg asked him.

Irsu listened. That sound was familiar. He slipped off his helmet to hear better. The sound echoed back and forth between the hillsides that surrounded them.

Finally he figured it out.

Somehow, the guards on the south side of the border had alerted their comrades further south. How, he didn't know. The humans weren't supposed to have magic.

"Run for cover!" he bellowed. A second later he was bolting for the tree line adjacent to the road, Coragg on his heels, most of the rest of Iron Company was doing the same.

Eight of the air machines ripped over, spitting their venom down on the road as the dwarves raced to cover. The six supply carts were helpless. Irsu watched as some of the lizards and donkeys pulling the carts and a few of the drivers slumped to the ground.

"Zein be damned!" he spat out. "Get your filthy hides into the forest!" he screamed at those of his company still struggling. Some were wounded and crawling on the ground, trying to reach safety.

"You are the right choice for the platoon leaders if I die," Irsu barked at Coragg as he ran from cover.

He looked to the right and the air machines were banking around as they'd done at the gate. He grabbed a soldier with wounds to his legs and began dragging him toward the trees.

The drone of the machines grew louder, and they spat at him. The gravel of the road erupted around him, around the wagons, and around his fallen. They ripped past again, yet somehow he was unwounded.

The lad at his feet looked up at him with dead eyes.

"You will *pay*," he said coldly to the machines as they headed south, preparing to swing around again.

"Irsu, NO!" someone, probably Coragg, screamed from the trees.

He unstrapped his crossbow and stabbed his axe spike into the roadway. He set the crossbow on the axe handle, then aimed carefully at one of the machines bearing down on him.

The crossbow emitted a cracking sound as it fired, the bolt flew straight at the center of the spinning parts. He saw everything in slow motion, until the first slug hit him in the arm. It spun him around, knocked him to the ground, and the speed of life returned to normal as the ground erupted right where he'd been.

He hurt like he'd been bitten by a hydra.

The machines, seemingly satisfied for the moment, roared over once again from the north, this time not spitting their death on him.

He lifted himself to his feet as the other dwarves cheered from the tree line, racing toward him to slap him on the back and scream in joy.

They pointed to the machine burning on a hillside a few kadros to the north.

Irsu smiled. The humans were putting up a good fight, he'd give them that. But their best, so far, wasn't good enough.

The dead were far too many. Another eighteen. Plus all the carts were out of service.

"Cut trees. Cut the carts up. We'll burn our dead here," Irsu ordered.

"What if they return?" Coragg asked.

"I think the last thing they'll expect is for us to stay in the same place," Irsu responded. "But we won't be long." He turned to the soldiers around him. "Burn them in their armor and burn any supplies we can't carry."

Coragg grinned, pleased with the order. He turned to urge the soldiers onward. "Bolts, food for a day, some spare armor parts. Hammers, chisels, and rock working tools go. Move it! You have five minutes."

Irsu grabbed one of his soldiers, Habbas. He remembered the man was an iron worker. "Warrior, I need your help. Find some tools, get this plate off my arm."

He showed Habbas the damage. The rerebrace covering his upper arm was ripped open, skin and some muscle mixed in with the shredded metal.

"That's bad," Habbas said.

Irsu kept his patience. "That's why I need you to get tools and get the plate off. We'll wrap the wound. And we leave in five minutes," he gestured with his hands toward the shredded supply wagons. "Go now, please."

Habbas came back with Coragg. Together they removed the plate from Irsu's arm as the commander bit down on leather to silence his pain.

Coragg spoke to distract him. "When you joined us, I had doubts. We all had doubts. But Irsu, nobody can call you The Fainter now. You will have songs sung about what happened here today."

"If we live," Irsu reminded him. "And all I care about is getting home to Iron Mountain."

"But we may be coming back here anyway," Coragg said. "This will be our home now."

Irsu glared. He was only a few weeks from finishing his hearth if his mother hadn't resold it by now.

"Like it or not," Coragg said, "you're not the king. You don't decide where we live."

"Yet," Habbas said. "But a few more stunts like that and you'll be royalty for sure."

Irsu pursed his lips and narrowed his eyes. "That's the last thing I want."

"Let's get to Nollen," Coragg said. "It's time."

"We are leaving the road, now that we have no wagons," Irsu ordered. "In that regard, the humans may have done us a favor. Cross country we will be unseen."

The sound of air machines echoed in the distance.

"Let's get moving, we can assemble our lines once we're under cover of the trees," Irsu said.

Iron Company disappeared into the pines, leaving their dead burning on the road. It was the best they could do until they scribed the fallen onto the Wall of Heroes back home.

Chapter 21 - Between the Grave and the Sky

May 29, 1940

The plan to return to the evacuated areas was risky, Harry knew. The reason they were evacuated was either the Germans, or more probably, the dead were seen in close proximity. Raiding such places was, however, the only way his squad was going to eat and stay supplied.

Timothy and Wilkes brought a dozen chickens into the farmhouse they were occupying for the night. Garrett and Jones, both the newest privates in the squad, were digging graves.

Whether by pact or the decision of the husband, the people who lived in this house didn't evacuate. Gathered around a Bible at the kitchen table, the man had used a WWI service revolver and did his family in. There were four dead including himself. Each shot in the head, effectively ending any chance they'd join the legions of the WWI dead.

Maybe they believed the stories of the apocalypse. Maybe they thought the Germans were committing atrocities. Either way, this French family was no more.

The men stacked the bodies outside, where the family waited to return to the soil from which everyone came. And everyone returned.

"I'm glad we dropped off the French woman before she saw this," Timothy said. "You think she'll be okay?"

Harry rubbed the bump on his head. "She's a survivor, that one. Best she moved south, not along with us."

Timothy sighed.

"We best get on with it," Harry said, gesturing toward the back door.

Other than Miller, who stayed in the house because Harry demanded he look for information on the wireless whenever possible, the men gathered around freshly dug graves to inter the corpses.

Harry wasn't religious, he hadn't been since his early teens. But the men were expecting him to say something. Since he'd cared enough to order the family buried instead of tossed in the barn, he should probably have words to go along with that.

When the men formed a semicircle around the four holes, Harry removed his helmet, and so did they.

"Things have changed in our world, in ways I don't think we're fully aware of yet. Some, and I think that's what these poor folks thought, believe it's the work of God. He isn't hearing our prayers anymore if that's the case, because we're burying two children here today. What sort of world is that?"

He was probably crossing a line, but the men didn't say a word in protest.

"Or maybe they simply didn't have the faith to see His plan through. We don't know what the future holds. Maybe the emptiness will come for us tomorrow. Maybe a crossbow bolt, maybe a skeletal fiend will seize and destroy us. Whatever happens, I will not go this path."

He gestured at the graves.

"All of you are good, strong, British men. You have families back home, Ma, Pa, or a wife and maybe kids even. I will fight for us to see them again. I will fight the Germans if I must, and I will fight the dead because I must. I will fight those short armored bastards that seem to be everywhere we go. Until my last breath leaves my body, I swear I will fight to get you home."

He looked up to see some of the men nodding. Whether they were agreeing with the concept of going home or the fight to get there, he had no idea.

"Whatever motivated this family, they gave up. We will not. But we will respect their choice and put them in the ground."

He waited as the bodies were lowered into the holes, then he walked a short distance away to speak to his men again.

"We can't go south anymore. In the villages that haven't seen the dead, we are cowards unworthy of aid. In the villages that have, no aid is spared. We are on our own. But there is hope. The way east, along the front of the dead men, we may find a path through to civilization. There is a truce. If we can meet up with the Germans on the other side of this line, maybe they'll spare a plane to get us home. If not... can anyone here fly?"

Everyone looked at each other, nobody raised a hand.

"Maybe I'll steal us a plane and fly us home myself. How hard can it be?"

The men laughed.

"Alright, that plan probably won't work. But this narrow corridor is all we have. We will have a guard at all times. We will have Miller listen. We will stockpile diesel and food. We have a great lorry, reliable and stout. We're intelligent British men made of the good stuff. So we will come through this if I have to drag every bloody thing that is coming through that gate down to Hell myself."

He was quiet a moment. "Garrett, Jones, put the French family to rest. Use their tractor to fill the holes. We've spent enough time on the needs of others who quit." He wagged a finger at the men gathered around. "That is not who we are. We are British soldiers. *We* do *not* quit."

"We do not quit," some repeated. Others shook their heads in agreement.

As he walked away Timothy stepped into rhythm next to him. "I'm not sure the men need their faith in God shaken."

"I don't need them looking to God for answers," Harry said. "I need them looking to me. Or to themselves. Because this," he stabbed a finger at his own head, "is where the answers are going to come from. One day at a time."

"You're in charge," Tim yielded. "I have seen men do more for God and Queen than anything else so far, however."

"The Queen can go straigh…" Harry took a deep breath. "I doubt the Queen has ever slogged through dead WWI soldiers, mystical creatures knee deep, and French families that committed murder-suicide."

"Probably not. Nobody has until now. Until us."

"Damned right. Which is why we'll deal with this as it comes." Harry shook a smoke from a pack he'd found in the house. "Want one?"

Timothy laughed. "I'm still smoking the packs you gave me when all this nonsense started."

They stepped into the house. Miller was in the kitchen with the radio on the table, along with some maps they'd found in an abandoned petrol station the day before. The Bible was on the floor. Harry would have left it, but Tim picked it up and sat it on the counter.

"Anything, Miller?"

"The Prime Minister gave a speech. It's to be repeated in a few minutes."

Tim went to the back door. "News on the wireless. Jones, Garrett, you have watch when you're done with that tractor."

Several men filed in. Harry and Timothy sat in chairs that a few hours earlier seated the dead. The kitchen was still a bloody mess, and the scent of blood lingered.

"Ladies and Gentlemen, the Prime Minister of England."

Time passed, and the scratch of a phonograph needle started.

"I stand before you, flummoxed. Last week I thought our greatest enemy to be the Hun. Now, while I don't know our enemy, I do know we face a threat like none we've ever seen. I know there are enemy ground forces I have no information about, and not the Germans. We've had reports of serpents in the Channel. Sea serpents, mind you, not garden snakes. Dragons in the sky over Canterbury and Manston, something our RAF has been struggling to deal with at great cost.

"I can tell you now, my fellow citizens, that I wasn't about to lay down for the Huns, and I'm not about to lay down for these invaders from beyond either. We have our soldiers scattered all over France by a wave of the dead which have risen up from WWI graveyards. We have limited and dwindling numbers of Spitfires and Hurricanes. We have ships being ravaged from beneath the water. But I assure you, oh England, that we have not yet stood to our full height! Our factories are tooling up to spit out aircraft in numbers like we've never seen. Our Navy will protect our ports, if that is what it takes."

Several seconds of silence.

"There is good news. The United States as agreed to help in our fight against the supernatural, and I'll tell you that was a story to sell the American President. If, and I tell you this to prove it can be done, we hadn't shot down one of these dragons, I wouldn't have had any proof. But I sent the head of that beast to Franklin Roosevelt and upon receiving it he came to see things were as I said. Add in the truce with the Germans, who had the sense to assassinate that madman Hitler, and I think we have a chance.

"This is good. American industrial might and the numbers of their men will help us make short work of these invaders. Together, we of the Commonwealth and citizens of the free world, we will fight back those who would take what is ours. Stand firm, stand proud, stand tall, but most of all, stand."

The radio announcer returned. "Now the weather—"

"He has no idea what's happening," Wilkes said, sneering.

"I don't know, mate, he sounded like he had at least a clue," Miller rebutted. "I think he's got much of the picture, he's just not sure how to deal with it yet. Who would be?"

"Just another bloody politician, that's what he is," Wilkes spat out. "What would he know of what we're doing?"

"Don't know if you know who the man is, Wilkes," Harry said, "But that's Churchill. You have two more wars to fight after this one to catch up to the man. He's seen his share."

They argued for a bit longer, it was the stress. But in the end the decision was it didn't matter. No supplies were coming. No reinforcements. No air drops. They were on their own until they found a solution to their situation.

"What if we went to this gate and, you know, flipped a switch or something," Parker suggested.

"Flipped a switch?" Wilkes scoffed.

"Maybe we could just turn it off," Parker replied.

"I think it's a grand idea," Harry said. "We'd be heroes to the world. But how do you suggest we break through the lines of dead along the Maginot? As soon as those codgy sorts see us, we're rightly screwed."

"We must cross it somewhere," Parker replied. "Who's to say where?"

"And don't you think there'll be more of the types we've been seeing? The red and black armor fellows?" Timothy asked.

"Not all bad," Jones said in response. "The red ones practically gave us kisses."

"And the black ones?"

Jones' eyebrows furrowed. "Yeah. Those ones. We need to find a way to kill those blokes."

"Tomorrow is a new day. Standard watch, we'll leave in twelve hours. It will be light, we'll be able to see."

"What's the village we're moving toward?" Wilkes asked.

"Esnes."

"What's there?"

"We'll know soon enough. It's not like I live here, Wilkes," Tim said. "Get some sleep, you have middle watch tonight."

Harry watched Wilkes leave the room, headed to find something soft to lay his head on.

"They're under pressure," Tim told him. "Each day a bit closer to the edge."

"Then we push them back from it, Timothy," Harry said. "We push them back."

Tim looked at him like he'd asked for the impossible.

"Every man on this team needs the others. We let nobody down."

Tim nodded. "I'll be up on the roof. There's a chill in the air, maybe some rain. Maybe with first watch I'll get the warmth back in my bones before my eyes open again."

"Wake me when you come down."

He watched Tim walk out the back door, then finished his smoke.

Rest never came easy. It wouldn't be easier with the ghosts of dead children and desperate parents haunting him.

Chapter 22 - Mockeries of Men

May 30, 1940

As the new day began, Harry awakened as rested as he'd felt in a long time. Most nights over the last week he'd given the men the better beds in whatever place they occupied, but this time Timothy had insisted they save one for him.

He hadn't argued. It was nice to feel free of muscle aches and stress.

This despite the horror that had occurred in the house sometime within the last few days.

Wilkes burst into the front room as Harry was tapping out his morning smoke.

"There are men approaching on horses from the north."

"Cavalry? Do the Germans have cavalry?" Harry asked, looking at Timothy.

"Their cavalry clanks a lot and shoots bits at us," Tim replied. "Hans would know."

Harry wasn't sure, Hans didn't seem like he was all that thrilled to be part of the Wehrmacht. Why else would he be running around France with a British squad? "He's searching the barn for anything useful. Wilkes, make sure everyone is under cover. We don't want to engage if we can avoid it."

Harry jumped up and grabbed his binoculars from his pack. He ran to the front of the house, then climbed to the roof. He dropped to his belly and slithered up to the peak of the house, which ran east-west. Well covered, the enemy shouldn't spot him.

As his head crested the ridge just enough to raise his field glasses to view northward, he was surprised by what he saw.

About two dozen men on horses over a mile to the North, riding the most ridiculously decorated horses he'd ever seen. Enough ribbons, heraldry symbols, and pomp to make King George feel overdone.

Tim scuttled up next to him. "What's the situation?"

"Men on horses, apparently having a parade." Harry handed the glasses over to his friend.

"Parade?" Timothy raised the binoculars, staring for over a minute. "If that's not the stupidest thing I've ever seen, I'll eat your socks."

"My socks are safe," Harry said, taking the glasses back. He raised them once more. "Get the men to the ready. I see bows, I see some pikes, and the lad with the most ribbons in his hair is sporting a sword of some kind. These aren't men of our world."

"Will do," Tim said as he slid back down.

He heard the men shuffling below as they prepared their weapons, Tim ordered the Hotchkiss set up on the kitchen counter, which had a window overlooking the north fields of the farm.

The men on horses, if they followed their path, would pass half a mile north of them headed west-southwest.

He studied them intently as they moved closer.

Suddenly one of the men, who wasn't a man at all, jogged her horse south straight toward him. His heart fluttered at how beautiful her face was. She was wearing what appeared to be some sort of leather armor, crafted as amazingly as the female that wore it. After forty yards or so she stopped, then stared right at him for a good minute.

He froze. Did she see him or one of the men?

She turned her head back toward the rest of her companions, who seemed entertained by her enthusiasm. Despite their smiles, they turned toward the farm.

The jig, as they say, was up.

"Tim," Harry yelled as he slid down from the roof. "Get ready! They've seen us somehow."

"Shall we shoot first?" he heard from in the house as he dropped to the ground.

"No, definitely not," he replied as he ran inside to the now set up Hotchkiss. "The red people were friendly enough, maybe we shouldn't risk a fight if we don't need one."

Timothy told the men to hold fire.

Several minutes passed as the horses slowly approached across the fields. Whoever these people were, they weren't in a hurry. When they stopped, the one Harry believed to be the leader stood near the fence that separated the back yard of the house from the fields.

His ears were pointed, and his facial features were too slender. Also, his skull was not quite the right shape to be human. He was something else. Otherwise, at a distance and despite his apparent lack of nutrition, he was very humanlike.

The fellow clutched at a medallion that swung decorously from his neck, over his remarkably intricate plate armor.

"Humans, our scout has seen you in the structure," the fellow began. "We will escort you to the gate."

Harry waited for him to say something more.

"Answer him," Tim urged.

"We're fine, thank you," Harry said. "We'll find our own way."

The person laughed. "That's not how this works. Move from the house, you will be treated well and given a new life in a new world."

"We rather like this one," Harry yelled out the window. "Move along, we'll do the same."

The fellow smiled, and Harry didn't like the condescension the smile included. "Have it your way."

The plated warrior rode back north to rejoin his group. A few minutes after that they stormed south together on horseback, after drawing bows, swords, and readying their lances for charging.

"Open fire!" Harry yelled.

He charged the Hotchkiss and opened up on the surging enemy. The results were far better than he'd hoped. The horses went down quickly, although the almost-men, whatever sort of abomination they were, did not.

Soon the enemy troops were on the ground, hiding behind what cover they could find, be it a tree, a fallen horse, or a decrepit wagon sinking into the dirt of the field.

"Hold your fire," Harry yelled.

Within a few seconds the gunfire ceased. A dozen horses and half a dozen of the manlike things lay motionless in the dirt.

"Leave now and the rest of you can live," Harry yelled.

"That's not how this works," their leader yelled back. "You've drawn Elistinar blood, and for that you must die."

"Are you sure you're aware of your tactical situation?" Harry asked.

"Your arrogance will change that soon enough," the leader replied. "Surrender and your deaths will be quick and merciful."

Good enough, that made the solution easier for Harry. "Men, fire only when you see a target. Save ammo, make it count."

For half an hour the standoff continued. Occasionally one of the horse people would stick their head up enough for Harry's crew to take a shot. Twice that resulted in a dead enemy. A few dozen times it resulted in a wasted bullet.

Harry was trying to figure out where the leader was. Maybe if he killed that one, the rest would demoralize and run.

A figure popped up from behind a dead horse. The person knocked an arrow, raised his bow, fired, and dropped back to the ground faster than Harry would have thought possible.

The arrow flew straight at his position, striking one of the top panes of glass in the kitchen window. Tim hadn't knocked the high panes out, as the gun fired below them.

The arrow blew glass into his and Timothy's faces, then bounced off his helmet before disappearing somewhere behind him with a loud thunk as it slammed into a wall.

His head hurt from the impact.

Several of the enemy popped up at once to attempt the same maneuver, but this time Harry's men were ready. They gunned most of the archers down, although he heard at least one of his men screech as he was hit.

"Damn," Harry said. "Give me a grenade, Tim."

He took the grenade and slipped to the back door. He quickly glanced around the corner to familiarize himself with the positions of the enemy. The cart was a good twenty-five yards away, he wondered how accurate he'd be.

As he drew his head back behind the door frame to ready the Mills bomb, an arrow raced past. A second earlier and it would have skewered his face. It slammed into a buffet that held the family's dishes, shattering things inside as it penetrated.

Harry didn't hesitate. Now was the time.

He stepped into the door and hurled the grenade. He leapt back to cover without waiting to see the results. He heard gunfire erupt from around the property, more than one of the enemy must have jumped up to shoot at him.

Two arrows plunked into the buffet, shattering more of the dishes within.

"Spot on, Harry!" Tim yelled.

The grenade exploded, and the battlefield grew silent for the moment.

A female voice called him next in some language he didn't understand. He'd have sworn she was singing had that fit the situation.

A second later she must have found whatever it was that allowed the fellow to speak.

"We will withdraw," she said. "We'd like to do so under a truce."

"If we see your kind again, we will fire first and ask questions after the fact," Harry informed her.

"You are right to put it that way," she replied. "You will not see us again."

Something in her voice didn't sound right. Something told him that she was planning him harm.

He looked out the window and raised his binoculars to study her. She was glaring in his direction with hatred like he'd never seen. It chilled his soul seeing her face, she somehow managed to mix unearthly beauty with a malevolent and vile evil that stunned him for a moment.

She had no intention of letting them go their own way.

"Open fire!" Harry yelled as he slipped behind the Hotchkiss. The gun erupted, and the female screamed as she fell behind the cart. Harry splayed the gun over the field of battle. Something guided him and his men, their bullets found their marks with remarkable accuracy.

It was at that moment he realized Miller was standing behind him, chanting something in a language Harry didn't understand.

The battle was over quick. The tide had turned, and the enemy, pinned down, had no escape. When the last six of the enemy broke and ran, Harry ordered his men to let them go.

He turned and looked at Miller but didn't ask any questions. He wasn't sure if he'd like the answer.

Instead he walked out to the field, to the cart to see the condition of the wounded.

The male leader was dead, his head punched through with grenade shrapnel.

The female was laying on the ground next to him, looking up at the sky.

"I never thought to die so far from home," she said, the malevolence gone.

Harry knelt next to her, checking her wounds. Shot through the lower torso in several places, her liver and lower organs were destroyed. Assuming these things kept them where humans did.

"You had no intention of letting us go."

She smiled, blood poured from the corner of her mouth. "One does not make deals with creatures such as you. Even the dwarves are more honest."

"The dwarves?" Harry asked. "The short men?"

"You insult them calling them men. Humans are vile," she spat out, coughing.

"Your intent to betray us at your first opportunity was written all over your face," he replied. "We're not the vile ones. You planned to slaughter us when our guard was down."

"You're not as stupid as you look," she laughed. "Who are you? I should know my killer when I move on."

"We..." a voice said from over his shoulder, "we are the Templars."

"Aaah," she responded, as if that explained everything.

A second later her eyes glazed over as her body gave up.

Harry had no pity.

He looked around the area. Jones was shot in the shoulder with an arrow, but it hadn't pierced anything vital it seemed. Timothy was pouring some liquor from the house on the wound, getting it ready to bandage.

Good, that problem was dealt with, and even better, Jones would live.

They needed to get moving, reducing risk from the ones he let go. Time to give the orders. "Take their food. These fallen horses, that's meat. Get as much as will last for a day. Look over their supplies, see if there is anything we can use. Wilkes, get padding in the bed of the Matador for Jones. Take a mattress from the house if you like. Hans, grab a few of these bows and a stock of arrows. We might need to start practicing with them."

Everyone turned to the task, but Harry wasn't done. "Not you, Miller."

Miller looked at him, resignation on his face. He knew he had some explaining to do.

"Let's go for a walk and have a talk," Harry added, gesturing toward the barn, away from the others.

"I suppose it's time," Miller sighed.

Chapter 23 - Iron Boxes

Irsu was in a war meeting with his scout and his second in command. They were camped in a stand of trees surrounded by farm fields. The camp was dark, no fires. The area they were in was too thickly inhabited to risk anyone detecting the light. A small lantern lit the tent, a risk Irsu deemed worthwhile for the sake of the meeting.

"There is a city to the southwest," Numo reported. "Their torches are amazing, you can see them for *dokadros*."

Irsu leaned on his axe. They'd covered the terrain between the border scuffle and their current position in two days. Light to heavy hills, but no real mountains yet. That was about to change.

"We need to come in from the south side of Nollen to reach the entrance," Irsu said. "What's the best way to go?"

"There's a lake south of the city, surrounded on three sides by mountains. In fact, Commander, all the low points around here have lakes, or if not lakes, streams or rivers."

"It won't be easy traveling, then," Irsu said, finishing Numo's implied conclusion. "But we have one thing in our favor, the humans like to build bridges."

Coragg frowned.

"You don't like that?" Irsu asked him.

"We saw the result of traveling on the road. Like it or not, the humans pack a sting. Their spitter sticks are vicious."

"And if we use their bridges we risk being smashed by their machines," Irsu admitted. "With your thought in mind, we make our own way. That's probably wise, Coragg."

Numo gestured toward the map they'd seized at the border post and made something of a grunting sound.

Scouts were strange.

Irsu handed him the papers and Numo spread them out on the ground.

"This is where we are, roughly, almost due north of our goal. If we go to the south end of this lake here," he pointed at the map, "we can take this valley to this location," he moved his finger to a new spot, "and Nollen's face will be a ten or twelve *kadros* south from there."

"It's a good way," Coragg agreed. "Does it have river crossings?"

"The map doesn't say, so probably not a major river," Irsu replied. "We can go this way, although we will be exposed if there is no tree cover."

"It is the only way unless you intend to swim a lake and climb several peaked ridges to get there," Coragg replied.

"Alert the platoons," Irsu agreed. "We rise early to pass this city in the dark. There is no need to attract human attention to ourselves."

"I'll get the word passed," Coragg agreed and disappeared from the tent.

True to his intention, they were moving again two hours before the sun. It was hard on the troops to march in the dark. Visibility was already bad enough from their helms, and the darkness created even more problems. They moved at half speed to ease the difficulties.

By sunrise, or at least by the time the sky was growing light, they were on the south side of the lake and headed east. A small village nestled against the southern shore, but thick habitation stretched up the valley to the south.

It would be hard not to be seen. Diverting south would only add time to their journey, without helping them stay hidden.

Irsu decided to just march through the village, the far side looked like more farmland, then a steep ridge line past that. The slope up to the ridge was covered in trees, blessed cover they'd need to survive. They'd make for those to lose the humans once again.

That plan had already worked once.

Other than some screams, they encountered no issues passing the village. The inhabitants who noticed them slammed their shutters, and after initial cries were quiet.

The soldiers reached the trees just as some of the air machines began sweeping over the farm fields, undoubtedly looking for Iron Company.

The climbing was difficult. Not steep enough to need serious equipment, but steep enough that it was dangerous to fall as one of his soldiers proved. A broken neck. Another dead.

Soon, however, the ground leveled off and opened up to farmland once more. Irsu sent two soldiers south with their dead companion with orders to build his pyre away from the main body of dwarven troops. Hopefully the ruse would solve two problems.

Burn the dead and fool the humans.

"They know roughly where we are," Irsu said to Coragg. "It's just a matter of time before they send in ground forces." He removed his helmet, Coragg did the same. "But hear their air machines? The moment they spot us they'll be spitting death at our platoons again. We've lost enough."

Numo was scouting, and Irsu could wait for him to come back with a way, but time was precious when being hunted.

"We go south," Irsu ordered. "I think I see thicker trees down that way. It's also away from the decoy pyre."

They traveled south along the ridge, staying in the tree cover. Their armor, being silver, would normally give them away. But Coragg had ordered the warriors to smear themselves down with mud from the forest floor.

Soon not a piece of armor glinted, much to the dismay of the owners.

"We'll get to Nollen soon enough," Irsu promised. "Stop whining like the mules of a common merchant. You'll be able to clean and polish once we're safe."

"How are we going to keep the air machines off of us as we scale the face of Nollen?" a soldier asked.

"We'll deal with that then," Irsu answered. "We've already killed two of them. More will just decorate our legends."

The troops around laughed. That was the perfect answer for them, and they'd pass it around. Leading soldiers was as much politics as anything else. But the politics of soldiers used more lively language.

Numo rejoined them from their direction of travel. "You're going the way I would recommend. To the south the forest narrows to thirty *kadros* or so. We will do best to make haste at that point, I think."

"Your instincts are good," Coragg said to Irsu. "Or your eyes. Either way works."

"We have to move east soon," Irsu said. "We will lose soldiers to the air machines if they see us. How large is the stand of trees on the other side of this flatland? In the rolling ridges?"

"Extensive," Numo answered. "We will be able to stay in the trees for a long time."

"Then we move as far as we can today," Irsu said, "using trees as much as we can. Numo, you will move ahead, scouting the path that provides the most cover, reporting back every hour with an hour long march plan."

"Aye," Numo responded and disappeared.

Irsu turned to the nearest of his soldiers. "We're moving. Pass the message back along the column. No rest for the weary today."

They moved as silently as a company of armored troops could, but Irsu still believed it was only a matter of time before the humans found them.

A small clearing ahead of them housed a few hundred troops. And two large metal boxes with the largest spitter sticks Irsu had seen yet.

"And so it gets hard," Coragg said. "Why does it always have to get hard?"

"They haven't seen us yet," Irsu replied, ignoring the actual question. "Although I don't know how, our company is loud like the war gongs in the Hall of Warriors."

"They are wearing metal."

"I didn't say I blamed them." Irsu stared across the field at the war boxes. What were the capabilities of those things? "I doubt a crossbow is going to stop those."

"I'd say not," Coragg agreed.

"We camp here and move at dark," Irsu replied. "With our armor mudded, they'll not see us a *kadros* away."

"I'll let the platoons know."

"They camp in their armor, speaking in whispers, no fire, cold food only," Irsu added. "We take no chances."

Coragg looked at him like he was stating the obvious. Which he was.

"You have to give these humans credit," Irsu said to nobody in particular after his second left to his duty. "Armoring several warriors at once is a good idea… imagine that thing with a proper ballista on it."

"You giving orders, sir?" a passing soldier asked.

"Not yet, lad." Irsu grinned.

If he made it out of here he was going to change the nature of war thanks to the things he'd learned from the humans.

Chapter 24 - Film

May 30, 1940

Much to Ernst's dismay, Bad Münstereifel didn't have a dark room capable of processing the film taken aboard the HS-130.

The cartridges of undeveloped data had to be flown to Berlin, developed, and then flown back. A frustrating three day delay.

Ernst used every second, however. He put his team to work researching the artifacts of history, particularly of the two world religions that gave rise to Western power. If the artifacts of the other religions were so great, why didn't they help protect those areas of the world from European domination?

He had a few leads from the men and women he'd assembled to recover his legacy. Several of them suggested the Ark of the Covenant, although few of them agreed on where it was or even if it still existed. Ernst felt he knew better. It existed. It was in Ethiopia.

Case closed in his mind, although he didn't come down on the matter with them so hard.

Ernst had another idea, one that would take him outside of the three main religions of Abraham. In ancient China a discovery existed that intrigued Ernst. He'd have gone to China a long time ago to recover these artifacts, but he'd just heard of them from Dr. Herta Spekt, one of his new team members.

She was phenomenal. Intelligent, yet devoid of care for the mundane emotions, Ernst was growing increasingly fond of her.

Her contribution to the team was knowledge of a collection of artifacts called the Dropa Stones. Estimated to be over 10,000 years old, the stones tell the story of a crashed flying ship crew that mated with the locals and eventually became a part of local mythology long after their deaths. Supposedly the stones were much like phonographic records, and with the right equipment would reveal the secrets of their creators.

According to Herta the information contained on the stones was partially decrypted by a British archaeologist in the last century and contained knowledge about how to travel between worlds.

It was possible the stones referred to gates such as the type created by the Intepna Hojarr and the Inshu Key.

He relished the thought of such a long trip with his research team, particularly with Herta. The intellectual conversations, the shared knowledge… it would be glorious.

Of course, the first priority was still the Ark of the Covenant, but if that research didn't produce fruit, maybe Herta's idea would.

Someone knocked on his door.

"Come," he said.

A technician in a white jumpsuit rolled a cart into the room.

"Herr Haufmann, the images are fresh from the plane. Dr. Spekt asked that I bring them straight here. She would like to join you in observing the images.

"I would like that," Ernst said, unusually pleased. "Please notify her as such."

"Heil, von Krosigk," the man said, snapping his arm into the familiar salute.

"Heil," Ernst responded ritually as he moved toward the cart. File boxes stored the images, categorized by time and angle from the aircraft measured in direction and side slant.

"Hello, Ernst," a familiar voice called to him.

Herta.

"Come in, Fraulein, I mean Dr. Spekt," he replied, aware of the stupid smile on his face.

"Herta is fine, Ernst, we are colleagues, not formal acquaintances."

He gestured toward the couch. "Please, have a seat. I will roll the cart up, sit beside you, and we can discuss the images. Coffee? Wine?"

"Wine, please. Half a glass."

He poured from a French bottle brought back from the front, or what was the front a week ago. Now it was a chaotic mess of rumor and nonsense.

He sat her glass on the end table, then his at the other end before sitting next to her. "I am most interested in the film from the time we were over Rotterdam's presumed location."

"Presumed?"

"That's right, you were not on the plane, having arrived in Bad Münstereifel after we departed," he remembered. "We did not find Rotterdam, it was not there."

"Not there?" she said, her face perplexed.

He was happy she didn't presume to say he was speaking nonsense. "The images will show all, my dear Herta, let us begin. You will be up to speed on the details of our mission by the time our study here is done."

They looked at the images for hours. Dinner was brought to them, a delicious roast made for the officers that staffed the bunker complex. He benefited from the fine dining flag officers often experienced.

When they finished dinner, they returned to the task, sharing conversation. Ernst told her about the dragon attack and how they seemed to have a maximum altitude. Useful information he'd passed on to the German High Command.

He told her about the magician on the tower, shooting what could only be a magic attack at their aircraft. The engineers looking over the prototype after their return were outraged that the team brought the plane back damaged.

They laughed together at the engineers. Did these men think combat aircraft would always be shiny and dust free?

"This one here, is of a German soldier, is it not?" Herta asked. "Standing next to the magician you mentioned?"

Ernst took the image. It began to shake in his hands. He felt his body trembling as rage built inside.

"MECKLER!" he exploded as he stood up. He raged around the room, careful not to damage the picture, but a lamp and a few small trinkets on tables were not so lucky.

Two SS soldiers with MP-40s rushed in. "Is there a problem, sir?"

"GET OUT!" Ernst raged.

During his loss of control Herta sat calmly on the couch, continuing her work of examining the photographs.

Finally, Ernst was spent. Meckler was a traitor to the Fatherland.

"I have more images of him if you need proof for the generals," Herta said. "I think this makes it quite clear that Meckler is the villain here, not you."

He turned to stare at her. That was a very good angle. But he didn't want his commission back. He wanted more power, the power that would come from appointed office.

"You have already been more aid to this cause than that sycophant was the entire time he worked with me," Ernst said. "I admire someone with your composure."

She stood up and walked in front of him, drawing close. "You were justified, Meckler is a traitor. I am outraged as well, but as a woman my indignity is demonstrated differently. My father was passionate about Germany as you are."

He had never met a woman like her. "Your understanding is all I could ask for."

She placed a hand on his suit jacket, splaying out her fingers across the fabric. "I know I am not long in your life or on your team, but I don't see anyone else applying for the job." She looked at the floor then back up at him. "I would like to replace Meckler, but you can rest assured, Ernst, I am both loyal to the Fatherland and to those who gift me with opportunity."

He was flushed with excitement at her touch. The woman was intoxicating. "I had not thought to have another second in command," he said softly.

"I've overstepped my bounds," she said, turning away. "I'm so sorry, you have so much to think about and here I am—"

"Nonsense," Ernst said. "You're right, I need someone to be my voice when I am not here. Or help me on the journeys. This task is too great for one man."

She turned back toward him, her face lit up. "I don't think you aren't up to the task at all. I just want to help, Ernst Haufmann, and I believe I would serve your needs perfectly."

He grabbed her arms and drew her to him. Their kiss was long, warm, and unlike any he'd felt before. "Then it is done," he told her. "You will replace Meckler, and together we will close this gate the traitor opened upon the Reich's territories."

Her perfect lipstick was smudged slightly from their embrace. "We will, Ernst. We will make it right and find greater power for the Reich."

"For the Reich," he said as he pulled her close again.

Her fingernails dug into the back of his neck with just the right amount of pain.

They were going to go far together as a team. They'd close the gate with Meckler on the other side, leaving him there for eternity. And maybe just enough of the fantastical otherworldly enemies on this side to keep the Allies off guard and allow Germany to return to their just war.

Chapter 25 - The Fire of the Templar
May 31, 1940

Wilkes was in back of the Matador for a change. Miller, Timothy, and Harry sat in the front where they could discuss issues at hand.

"Tell Corporal Martin what you told me," Harry demanded.

Miller looked uncomfortable, like he was revealing the secrets of the King himself. "My family has been associated with the Templars, an ancient order of knights, for hundreds of years. Since the age of betrayal, when several knights escaped the slaughter of Jacques DeMolay and the seizure of Templar assets."

"What the blazes are you talking about?" Tim said, laughing.

"Tim, listen to him," Harry insisted. "He's got the juice to back it up."

"My great grandfather was a part of the founding of the Sovereign Military Order of the Temple of Jerusalem last century, near to 1800," Miller explained. "But that was just the public rebirth of an order that had been underground for centuries, and stretched back far past public knowledge of the Templars in the 1200's."

"You've both gone loony," Tim said. "Bad liquor at the last stop, maybe?"

"Show him," Harry ordered.

Miller, sitting in the middle, raised his hand. A deep chill entered the cab despite the open front windshield as he began his effort, and a tiny glow appeared over the palm. Soon the glow became a roiling ball of fire a few inches in diameter, turning in on itself in a constant roil of heat and energy. Frost began to appear on the windows, and the breath of the men created wisps of clouds.

Timothy stopped the lorry and jumped out onto the country road. "What in the blazes was that?" he yelled.

The men in the back spilled out to see the concerning matter. Even Jones, who was feeling much better although his arm was still out of commission.

"The jig is up, Lieutenant," Miller said, his display no longer in effect. "We might as well show them all."

"Give me a minute," Harry said, alarmed. He'd counted on Timothy's discretion, apparently that had been asking a lot. He had a few choices. Throw Tim under the wheels and make the men think he'd lost his mind or take the chance that the men would be able to handle Miller's display of... well, witchcraft was the term that came to Harry's mind.

Tim was his friend. Once considered, betraying him was out the question. He really liked Miller, but they weren't close like he and Timothy.

"Over here," Harry ordered the men. "Form a circle around me."

Once they did, Harry pushed them back a few yards. To give Miller room, and to make sure nothing physical happened.

"Miller, here with me," Harry ordered. "We're going to get this all out in the open."

The puzzled looks on the faces of the men amused Harry and would have been a lot funnier if the situation wasn't both so strange and serious.

"Before this starts, the first man to take any action against Miller will get my boot in his arse," Harry said. "He's a vital part of this team, the only one that can get a sensible word out of that damned wireless, and we can't spare him. So if you're unable to handle what you're about to see, Dunkirk is that way." Harry pointed toward what he thought was the right direction. "Good luck."

That threat made the men's faces much more stern. Now they knew something was about to happen that would threaten their unity.

Harry unhooked the flap of his sidearm. "Now then, Miller. Get to it."

Miller raised his hand and once again the glow started over his palm. Soon the small sphere of fire was roiling once more. Harry noted that unlike in the confined cab of the Matador, he didn't really feel the temperature change much around him.

The men said nothing other than a few surprised expletives. Nobody wanted to hoof it to Dunkirk, especially not through a line of the dead, but Harry could see a mixture of fascination, horror, and disbelief in their faces now.

"Something's awakened in this world," Harry said, "and Miller's a conduit. Not a fault of his, but he's maybe one of the first to realize it. Maybe some of you could do the same."

Roughly half of the men put their palms out, Harry almost laughed at the looks of concentration.

"I've got more you haven't seen, Lieutenant," Miller said. "It might be useful."

"Do it then," Harry said. "Let's have it all."

Miller swiveled away from the group's half circle and raised his hands in a cup pointed toward a broken down carriage house on the side of the road.

The ball of fire shot from the center of his cupped hands, growing as it did so. When it hit the carriage house, it was a few yards across. Dimmer, roiling less violently, but with a lot more volume.

The raging orange sphere struck, then flowed over the building, like a drop of water might strike an absorbent sheet of paper. It was as if the fire was something the carriage house needed. The entire structure was in flames within a few seconds.

"Holy mother of Jesus," Garrett exclaimed from behind him.

"That's an affront to God," Harry heard someone else say.

He spun around. "Miller's on our side," he said angrily. "He's one of ours. You don't know God isn't giving him that ability, and for the first time in my life I can honestly say I might have seen something that proves the bloke exists."

Nobody said anything.

"If you have a problem with Miller's new ability, or abilities, then as I said, that way to Dunkirk. As I see it, in a world gone mad, at least some of the madness can be put to work by us."

Lars Henry, a young private from the northern isles of Scotland, spoke. The kid didn't say much, it was some effort for him to speak and be understood. "If tis witchcraft, then guid fur us," he began. "Yin mair gibble against oor enemies."

"What did he just say?" Jones asked.

"Witchcraft is good for us," Wilkes answered. "Another tool against our enemies."

"He's right," Harry continued, affirming Henry's statement. "We need all the help we can get." He looked at Miller, who looked drained if Harry was being honest, something that helped form his next statement. "I don't know how often Miller can do this trick of his, or any other he might learn, but imagine how useful that would have been against the pointy ears at our last engagement."

Nods. It was hard to deny that logic.

"Miller is one of us. He's been honest with us, even beyond my expectations. Therefore, we'll be straight with him. That's why anyone who can't handle what he can do, you can go out on your own. We'll give you supplies, your equipment, and wish you well."

It was the third time Harry had offered to break up the unit. Still no takers. He was pleased. "You've had your chance," he continued, "and you chose to stay. The first one to give Miller a problem, I'll be dealing with you harshly. Do you understand?"

Nods. More than a few of the men looked excited by the events of the night. Maybe they felt like Miller offered them more security. Harry wasn't sure yet, but that burning trick would certainly be useful in a battle. He wondered if it would make a man, or the dead for that matter, as hungry to burn as the carriage shack had been.

The shack was engulfed now, and flames raged toward the sky.

Harry waved toward the lorry. "We're a beacon to every nasty about. Load up, we're going to get down the road."

Two minutes later they were heading toward the east again. The same three men sat in the cab.

"Timothy, what's on your mind?" Harry asked.

"Lots of things," Tim replied. "I'm nervous. But I see the benefits of Miller's new talent too. Cooking might be easier."

Harry laughed. "Might be."

He looked over at Miller, who was smiling. Clearly the revelation had unfolded better than the lad had expected. "Can you teach anyone else the tricks?" Harry asked him.

"I'm not sure. It's more of a feeling than a conscious intent."

"Well, if you can or can't, we're better off than we were a day ago. Fire is a powerful thing."

"It is," Miller agreed.

"Lighting smokes will be easier too," Tim said, still thinking of uses.

Harry laughed. They were going to make it to whatever destiny life had planned for them. And he was more and more certain that destiny was a positive thing.

It was time to get on with it.

Chapter 26 - The Toll

"You scouted all night?" Irsu asked.

"There will be time to rest at Nollen," Numo replied. "Most of our way is forest. We will be exposed mainly when we get to the mountain."

"Then we should get started," Irsu replied.

"I'll tell the company to expect a hard day's march," Coragg said. "Will we stop at all?"

"Only if we must," Irsu replied. "The prize is in sight. We will feast when it is in our hands."

Coragg left to rouse the soldiers for marching. Irsu heard surprisingly little grumbling, at least from the nearby troops.

Looking from the tree cover out over the plateau of fields, there were even more humans, and now four of the armored boxes with big spitter sticks.

"We stay hidden," Irsu advised Numo. "We will progress single file, and every step of every soldier will be on a spot your feet have chosen." He gestured toward the south for Numo to get moving. "So choose well."

They set off along the edge of the plateau, for any human to see them that person would need to be not only at the edge of the level ground looking down on them, but also some distance into the pine trees.

With the light returning to the sky, the drone of the air machines returned as well. The humans deserved credit, they were searching very hard for the dwarves.

Unfortunately for the humans, this was the dwarves native type of terrain. They knew how to remain unseen and knew how to both surprise an opponent or sneak around an opponent.

Today they'd be doing the latter.

Numo had done wonders in the dark. Irsu, at the front with only Numo ahead of him, saw the work of the scout. He gained a cartload of respect for the strange dwarf. The trail was clearly marked, with scuffed bark, overturned stones, or bent twigs. Soon Irsu was learning to pick out the path before Numo took it.

This was a skill that would prove useful if they were ambushed and Numo went down. After an hour they were now east of the human encampment, having circled them from the south. They were climbing higher into the mountains, and Irsu's lungs felt unburdened with too much air for the first time in days.

"Ahead the first ridge of many," Numo whispered to him.

Irsu didn't pass that along. The troops would find out soon enough.

"The humans will send troops into the trees," Coragg said. "They can't leave this cover unsearched for long, if their commander has a trace of sense in his head."

"I'm aware," Irsu replied.

"I'm saying you should not be in front."

"And I'm saying I'm aware of your concerns," Irsu snapped back at Coragg before taking his next step forward.

"Stubborn mule."

"Aye," Irsu agreed.

Coragg was right about part of the equation. The humans did send troops into the forest. But their methods of confrontation differed from the dwarves, something of a lesson that Iron Company would learn in a few moments.

Air machines could be heard overhead, but also a sound in the distance, repeated over and over. As if a host of miners dropped their hammers into a chasm, striking nothing until the bottom.

Whump, the sound so softly came to them. Whump. Whump.

Three breaths later the forest erupted into fire and exploding ground.

"Disperse, meet a *kokadros* to the east," Irsu yelled toward Coragg.

Numo and Irsu raced forward even as the ground surged and rolled with the force of the barrage. This was far more significant than the artillery of the Iron Mountain clan, catapults that hurled trade wagon sized rocks over a valley.

His respect for the deadliness of the humans continued to grow. They were killing his troops without risking their own. Even as the tactic was applied to his company, Irsu had to admit this was a good way to do it.

The bombardment lasted several minutes. He and Numo raced together through it all. He would have to protect the scout if at any point their path served up a meeting that descended into personal combat.

The sound of dwarves screaming was unnerving, if Irsu was honest. Usually in battle, most dwarven warriors died silently, but this was something beyond comprehension to his troops. Looking back into the fray, Coragg advanced with a team of three from Hearthstone platoon as debris rained down on them.

"Numo, we wait for Coragg. We have a company, but I fear we soon will be but a squad. Let it be Coragg that joins us."

"Aye," the scout answered.

Irsu marveled at the lack of fear in Numo's face or voice. The dwarf was unfazed that this might be his last moment. Irsu's opinion of the scout rose again.

After Coragg joined them, they proceeded northeast along the forest. Irsu was sure that area was dangerous, as it was where the enemy would likely maintain the barrage, but to go out in the open fields would give the air machines the targets they sought.

There was no winning path, just the one they were taking that offered them a sliver of hope.

The bombardment was random. The will of the Gods would determine who lived, and who died.

At last the five dwarves were east of the barrage, with only one minor injury. That injury would have been worse if not for the soldier's armor.

Over the next twenty minutes a trickle of the company's warriors joined them. Many others died in the forest. Some others died as they fled the forest trying to escape the clutches of unseen lethallty, only to be struck down in the open fields by the armored spitter boxes or air machines.

When the attack was done, seventeen soldiers stood with him. Six were wounded, but all could travel.

"We stick to the trees, we move as fast and light as possible," Irsu told them. "Ditch everything but your breastplates. We will come back for them later, if the humans don't have them, but the armor is slowing us down. And possibly showing the air machines our location."

"This was my father's armor at the Battle of Wannoth!" one dwarf complained.

"If it's that important to you, keep it," Irsu offered. "But then your path is not ours. You will go south or north, not east with us."

The protester stripped his armor off, burying it under pine needles.

The others followed suit, hiding their valuable protection as best they could. Like Irsu, the armor was a significant portion of their wealth. He marked the tree in his mind that sheltered his, then swore he'd be back for it.

Once again, they mudded what remained of their armor. Irsu didn't know if it was glinting armor that gave them away, but if it was the cause of the barrage then the price for such attachment to a material thing was unbearably high. Over a hundred of his troops were either dead or wounded enough they'd soon be captured.

"Let's go," he said.

They fell back into a single file line.

"Step in step," Coragg warned those behind him. "They must not know our numbers when they find our trail. Or they will lose caution, and we will lose all."

Wise words.

No further attack happened on them following the bombardment, the humans were probably searching the barrage area even at that moment. It would take some time for them to determine the nature of their enemy, and by then Irsu would be far away.

Not long after they set out again the air machines stopped circling the area. Maybe the humans believed them all dead. Maybe creatures as weak as the humans would have been. But dwarves were made of stone, not butter.

The day's travel was long, but soon Nollen appeared in the eastern sky, growing larger with each ridge they crossed.

By the end of that same day they were at the base of a long snowfield that swept up the mountain to the top.

"I hadn't planned on us coming from this side," Irsu said. "But it will have to do."

"Can we get to the door from above?" Coragg asked.

Numo nodded. His confidence had grown once he'd arrived in the mountains. "I will find a way."

One of the wounded soldiers, Hobrith, had developed an infection during the day's march. Irsu checked on him as the soldiers dug cavities into the snowpack for their squad to rest in.

"Dig a deep hole for him," Irsu told two of the troops. "And get some wood from the tree line. He will have a small fire to heat his body and help fight the infection."

The deep hole would hide the light from the fire, and a small fire would turn the walls to ice, helping to keep the warmth in. The temperature at which water froze was very comfortable if wind was kept at bay.

"We rest here, we check our wounds, we assess where we stand in the morning."

Coragg looked concerned. "Do we leave him if he's deeper into illness?"

Irsu shook his head no. "Not a chance. We lose no more. If he dies, he will die in the Lost Hold, so he can celebrate his victory with his ancestors."

Coragg smiled. It was the answer he'd hoped for, clearly. "I'll see to it. If he lives the night, he'll enter with us."

"If he dies, he still enters with us. It's the right thing to do," Irsu added. "I am tired of doing what is wrong."

"Don't blame yourself for today," Coragg replied. "I have never seen anything like that attack. I hope I never do again."

"They've lost their chance. Tomorrow we make the summit, then the gate to the hold. Nothing will stop us now."

Coragg handed him a skin, which Irsu assumed was water. It was not. The sear of Iron Mountain whiskey stabbed Irsu's throat.

"You've been saving this?"

"To celebrate our entry," Coragg confirmed. "But I came too close to Ekesstu's grasp today. I'm not passing on with whiskey on my person instead of in my belly."

Irsu laughed and handed the whiskey back. "Save at least a drink for the hold. I will have it there if you don't think yourself worthy."

Coragg frowned but put the skin away.

"Tomorrow," Irsu promised. "Tomorrow is ours."

"Tomorrow," Coragg affirmed.

Chapter 27 - Resolution

June 1, 1940

"Lieutenant, we're north of most of the battles of WWI," Miller said. "What are the chances we could head north and take a look at this gate? If one had a mind to, I mean."

Harry looked over at the radioman. So far, the kid had known about the swords and about the WWI battlefields. He was doing magic. And, it turns out he came from a family descended from Templars.

"It's a good idea," Miller said after Harry ignored his first comment. "Might even help the war effort if we can get home."

"The chances are zero. Because I don't see any dead men around me right now," Harry said. "And I quite like that. A lot."

"If we keep heading east we're going to hit the Maginot line. If you think there aren't dead there, you're mistaken." Miller said. Quickly adding, "Sir."

Damned kid, Harry wondered if he wasn't too smart for his own good. Or maybe Miller should've been an officer. "What's our fuel?" Harry asked Tim, who was driving.

"About twenty gallons, we'll have a need soon."

"Let's stop and look at the map," Harry offered. "If north looks best, then we'll go."

They stopped once more on a country road, mostly gravel. Stone fencing lined both sides, to the south was rolling plains, to the north a forest stood off in the distance. East and west were hidden by the rise of gentle hills.

"Stay in," Harry said to the men, "unless you need a tree. We're checking the map for a course."

Groans from the bed of the lorry. "We've had our bottoms beaten flat," someone said.

"Beat them concave then," Harry replied as he spread out the map.

"Look here, we just passed Neuvilly," Miller said. "If we turn around we can head north there, and there will certainly be fuel in Valenciennes."

"How do you know that?"

"Because the radio said the Germans hold it," Hans translated. "Apparently my countrymen have stood hard against the invaders there."

"Why would they give us fuel?" Harry asked, irritation in his tone. "Why not just take our lorry and make us help defend the town?"

"Because we're allies now?" Miller said meekly.

"No," Harry said. "The Germans might not be fighting us, but we're not allies. We're just in a truce until this outworlder problem is solved."

"But what's to the east?" Timothy asked. "The kid is right. We're running straight toward Switzerland, and they'll never let us cross the border."

Harry sighed. "You too, Tim?"

"None of us want to go further from home, Harry. We want to get back to England. The south is no longer an option since the news of the dead isn't really taken seriously yet. Spain is out, they just got out of their own civil war. Can you imagine us driving through in British uniforms?"

Harry laughed. "Bloody cold reception that would be."

"Then we have to go to the French Mediterranean, if you don't want to visit Italy or Germany."

"I get it," Harry replied. "We're going north. But I'm not going to any German held enclaves and expecting a warm reception. We'll continue as we have, day to day, getting fuel and food where we can."

"Speaking of food," Wilkes said, standing up in the bed of the truck and pointing.

To the north side of the road was a single cow. How it had survived the Germans, the dead, and the other sorts running around, Harry had no idea.

"Shoot it," Garrett said.

"No," Harry snapped, but it was too late.

Wilkes' gun retorted, and the sound echoed out from their location. The cow dropped to the ground.

Harry shook his head in disbelief. "Wilkes, if you shoot without my order again, I'll take your gun away and make you carry all the gear."

"It's food, Lieutenant."

"Quiet, all of you," Harry shot back, irritated. "I mean it Wilkes. Don't disobey this order."

Wilkes looked down, embarrassed. He nodded his understanding.

Harry studied the map to determine a path to the north, when the men started yelling. So much for quiet.

He looked up to see four creatures in the field north of them, running toward their position. As they passed the cow, a good two hundred yards from the lorry, one stopped to pick it up. And did so with ease. The beasts, somewhat man-like, were the giants from Norse legends if anything ever was. Towering into the sky, three of the beasts kept coming for the lorry.

"Open fire!" Harry yelled.

The men were ready. A hail of bullets rained on the creatures, which slowed them down, but didn't kill them. If anything, the largest of them seemed angrier. As it neared the fence Harry prepared himself for the carnage that was about to unleash on them.

That's when Miller proved his true worth to the team.

An orange and ragingly bright ball of fire raced from behind Harry, straight toward the chest of the mighty monster. It impacted as the creature was crashing through the stone fence only a dozen yards from the lorry. The heat from Miller's trick was intense. Harry felt it from his position.

The ball of energy was a few yards wide when it struck the creature, and immediately it spread out over his torso. Much like the carriage house, the giant seemed eager to catch on fire.

The brute dropped to the ground, screaming, as the fire grew both inside the giant and outside as well. Flames licked from within the huge chasm of a mouth as the thing screamed, also unleashing a thick black smoke from the orifice like a smokestack.

The other three creatures, slower to arrive, froze in their tracks.

The two furthest away turned and ran back the way they came toward the trees.

The one with the cow flung it half the distance between him and the lorry as his burning compatriot stopped moving and succumbed to death.

Hurling the bovine at them was a futile attempt to bombard Harry's crew. With a cow. The last giant facing them peered across the field as if wondering what to do. It looked back at the two behind it, back at the Brits, then back and forth a few more times.

"Concentrate your fire on the standing one," Harry ordered.

A moment later the beast was writhing as a hail of bullets impacted his body. He gyrated like a dog being bitten by fleas, then turned and ran after his companions.

Harry looked at Miller. "Well don—"

Miller's eyes rolled back in his head and he dropped to the ground.

Harry burst into action, grabbing his soldier and lifting him toward the lorry. "Get him in the back, we have to go before they return."

"The cow!" Wilkes protested.

Obviously, Wilkes was hungry. Another issue to resolve.

"Run out there and cut off a back leg while we turn the lorry around," Harry ordered. "We're going back to Neuvilly for the night. It seemed abandoned, and the dead weren't swarming it."

It took a bit of time to sever a hindquarter, but it was worth it. They had a good amount of meat in a time when they were struggling to find food. Miller was breathing, although unconscious in the back. The Matador was facing west for a change.

They possibly had a mission, although nobody at any HQ had sanctioned it.

Their actual mission, to rescue British citizens, was a bust. Not a single one was found, alive or dead, during their travels. So a new mission might not be a bad idea.

Harry stared at the north forest line as the lorry bounced along. The giants were nowhere to be seen, but the more distance between them and his team, the better.

"Every day we see dragons in the distant sky. We see dead men walking the land. We see strange people who aren't human. And now giants? The world is mad," Tim said to him as they drove.

"It's not our world that's mad," Harry answered, "at least not in the way you mean. But the one that is spilling into ours."

Silence for a bit.

"Maybe Miller's right. We need to go north, get some intel, and get it home to the people who make decisions," Tim suggested.

"I agree. We'll make a plan in the morning, you and I. And Miller, I suppose. That lad's smarter than I ever knew." Harry sighed. "But then he's said more since the day this all started than he'd said in the time I'd known him before that."

"Strange kid," Tim said. "But he knocked down that monster when we needed it."

"Sacrificing himself," Harry agreed. "That's not going to work. We need heavier equipment if we're going to keep this up." He threw up his hands. "Giants? Really. Giants."

Timothy laughed. "It's preposterous."

"Damned right it's preposterous." Harry shook his head. "But it's also a fact. We're doing the best we can."

"We're alive."

"Yeah, Tim. We're alive."

Chapter 28 - The Ark of the Covenant

June 1, 1940

"Behold, the LORD thy God hath set the land before thee: go up and possess it, as the Lord God of thy fathers hath said unto thee; fear not, neither be discouraged," Ernst read to Herta from the Bible.

"You think that means God is telling man not to fear those who we are fighting now? That he was one of the powerful beings who created things like the gate?" She looked puzzled.

"I think exactly that," Ernst said, "although I admit, that's reading a lot into it. But I think there are ways to overcome the barrier, the Intepna Hojarr being one, in conjunction with the Inshu Key."

"What happened in Rotterdam, Ernst? I see the coldness that comes into your eyes when you speak of the gate. You were there, tell me."

"I had no idea what would happen, to be honest. We, our team, were setting up the Intepna Hojarr on the altar at the cathedral. Just as planned. We were to test the key, to see what effect it had step by step. By which I mean we were to turn it just a bit, and see what worlds opened to us, in order to advance the power of the Reich."

"Go on," she said.

"Then Meckler asked if he could turn the key," Ernst told her. "I said yes, he knew the plan. A tiny turn, observe the results. Instead he turned the key to its fullest extent. The gate surged forth, pulling everyone near the altar in. I, and the driver of my car, I'm not proud to say… we ran for our lives. Monsters began pouring through the gate and slaughtering the occupying troops."

Ernst did his best to look guilt ridden. "I should never have handed Meckler the key. How he knew betraying us would work him into favor with those on the other side, I don't know. But I had the key, and I gave it to him."

Herta grabbed him, looked him in the face, then hugged him close. "This is not your fault," she asserted. "Even the high command knows this, or they'd have removed you from the picture."

"Meckler worked for me. I should have seen his betrayal coming. That is why I will work to fix this. And see the Reich comes out on top in the end."

"You are a hero of the fatherland in my eyes," she said. "I will stand with you."

"You are risking everything if I fail, Herta. I don't want that for you."

"You will not fail. We will not fail. We will secure the Ark and bring it to Germany. It will protect us and help us close the gate. If not, the Dropa Stones may have the answer we seek."

"Maybe so," Ernst agreed.

"All such artifacts should be in Germany," she declared. "We are the only race smart enough to control them and protect the world."

"Your voice and your words," Ernst whispered in her ear. "They are like poetry I've waited all my life to hear, without knowing I was hollow inside. You have filled me."

She looked up at him and they kissed. A passionate kiss between two people who'd finally found another who shared their values. The kiss was long, and she touched him inside, stirring things he hadn't expected to feel.

He glanced up at the couch in his office, desiring to consummate their relationship.

She had other plans as she broke free of his embrace. "Let's ready for the trip to Ethiopia. We can get a flight to Berlin in the morning, gather resources, and the entire team could be on the way by the end of next week."

He stood carefully, so as to not reveal his excitement for her company. "An excellent idea. It is the Ark that will close the gate, I am sure of it."

"Why so sure?" she asked. "Shouldn't we be prepared for other options if it doesn't?"

"It's so clear to see," Ernst said. "In the earliest versions of Deuteronomy, there wasn't monotheism. There was simply a demand that the Israelites would not worship other gods. It is only later that progressed into the God of the Jews being the only god."

"So?"

"Don't you see?" he asked. "This god of the Israelites, he closed off this place to the other gods. Using the Ark he built. Whatever the reason, that god wanted this world and the people in it to himself from the very beginning."

"And you believe in this god?" Herta asked.

"As my god?" Ernst scoffed. "No. I have no need for a god. Even if this god still exists, which I think unlikely, why does he not speak to us? No, I think he is dead for a long time now."

"Then why will this dead god's Ark work to close the breach?"

"Because the Ark still has power, whatever powers it." Her eyes were ravenous as they ate up his words. "But it grows weaker, which allowed the Intepna Hojarr to create this breech. If we can bring the Ark close, I think it will close the hole between our worlds and allow us, humanity, time to prepare for when the Ark fails completely."

"Brilliant," she gasped. "But what is to keep the breach from reoccurring in another location. Say South America."

"The Intepna Hojarr was needed to make this breach. Unless another such device exists, the Ark's protection will hold long enough for us to build our weaponry."

She smiled at him coyly, then walked to the door and locked it. She stared at him for a moment from there, smiling, then walked to the couch and sat down. She patted the cushion next to her. "I've waited a long time to meet a man as smart as you. Let us consummate what obviously exists between us."

He smiled an eager grin. A brilliant woman was aroused by intelligence. He'd need to remember that if this day was to be repeated.

Although at the moment repeating was a secondary concern.

The important thing, at that moment, was how the first experience with Herta unfolded.

Chapter 29 - The Door

They were at the top of Nollen. Below them the peak fell away at a ninety degree angle on two sides. Only the way they'd come sloped gently enough for a dwarf to walk. Their footprints from the walk up to the peak disappeared into the distance.

Mordain was with them. The sky held low clouds, the bottoms of which almost scraped the peak where they stood. The air machines of the humans would not harass them this day.

"Behind us, several *kokadros*," Numo said, his voice urgent. "Human soldiers ascend the ice sheet."

"For the love of silver, you can see that?" Coragg asked.

"You can't?" Numo replied.

"Silence," Irsu ordered. "Coragg, set up the ropes, get us down to the door. Make it so we can deny the humans our path down."

"As you command," Coragg replied. "We have just enough rope between us to get it done."

"Then you shouldn't be telling me. Show me."

Coragg turned toward the unwounded dwarves, selecting two. Within minutes the first rope was in place and they had disappeared over the brutally steep south side of Nollen.

Irsu looked over the edge. Snow clung to the granite, and it was a steep drop to where the door was supposed to be. If they could get within before the humans saw them, they'd be safe. No human, elf, orc, troll, gnome, or otherwise would be able to decipher the door from the markings. To them it would simply be another rock on the face of Nollen. This place was definitely dwarven, and definitely the place they were looking for since coming to Earth.

"Numo, you're with me." Irsu picked four more of the unwounded and started work on an ice berm from which to shoot behind. They worked fast and hard, even the wounded would be able to fire a crossbow. If something went wrong trying to get in, this is where they'd make the gray-blue humans pay dearly for the end of Iron Company.

A few hours later the trench was dug and the firing positions in place. One by one they moved the wounded into position, except for Hobrith.

Hobrith was going to die today. The gods had not seen fit to still his infection. Irsu intended it would be in the hold, but Coragg needed to hurry.

He ran to the edge and looked down. Rope disappeared over a ledge below. The ropes had loops every *sungat* or so, so that a dwarf could have a foot and a hand within. Below that ledge the faint sound of hammering reached his ears. Coragg was still working.

He dragged Hobrith to the edge and held the warrior's head up. "You made it, my friend," Irsu said to him. "The gods have seen you to the door."

Hobrith didn't answer. His eyes opened, and a gentle smile was all he gave in return to Irsu's statement.

"I will get you in the door myself," Irsu promised. "If you pass before then, I will burn you in the Great Hall of the Lost Hold."

Hobrith's eyes closed and Irsu felt the soldier's forehead. The heat burned in him. Hot enough that Nollen should be snow free it felt to Irsu.

Numo ran up to his position. "Two *kokadros*."

"When they are inside one, we will start our defense," Irsu promised. "Do not fire until I say."

"As you wish," Numo agreed.

Fortunately, the humans weren't that fast on the icepack. It was probably an hour later, although hard to tell with no sun, when Coragg appeared over the edge. "We are ready for you to open the door."

"Just in time, my friend. I will head down. Hobrith is going with me."

"You could fall carrying him."

"Then I fall," Irsu replied. "I have a promise to keep. Tie him to my back."

It was awkward, but after removing all the weight from Hobrith they could, he was tied soundly to Irsu's back.

"I see you next in Dwarven lands," Irsu said to Coragg.

"In Dwarven security, in Dwarven iron," Coragg finished the old promise friends made to friends when leaving for patrol.

Irsu stepped into the first hoop and grabbed the feed rope with his hands. He lowered himself to the first handhold. He repeated the process over and over until he dangled in the air over a wide gap in the mountain's face. Below was the ledge that led to the door. A loop at a time Irsu continued down, his weapons, his armor, and Hobrith weighing on him like anchors.

After what seemed an eternity, he felt the strong touch of stone beneath his boot. He looked up to see the next dwarf in line moving past the overhang into the air gap. There was no time to waste.

He inserted his hand into a crack in the rock, then climbed a short distance into the depression on Nollen's face. At the top of the crack was a small ledge. That was all that remained of the old doorway's landing after ten thousand years.

"I guess I should be grateful the doorway is still there," he grunted out as he lifted his burden upward.

It took twenty minutes or so, but he made the ledge. By now six dwarves waited on the ledge below. The wounded ones. Coragg had sent them first.

Irsu pulled a small device from a pouch at his side. Given to him long ago by the priest of Ekesstu in Iron Hold, he'd kept it with him. He mentioned it to nobody other than Coragg, who would have taken it and opened the door if Irsu fell in battle. Not even Bordnu had known of the key, because Veznik was afraid his brother would take it from Irsu. The vision didn't allow for that.

The vision didn't allow for Coragg to open the door either, but Irsu only had so much faith regarding visions and other mystical nonsense.

Turns out this time the vision was right.

The key was an iron rod, about a hand long. Veznik told Irsu to simply plunge it into the stone of the door, no concern for where as long as it hit the door itself.

Irsu jabbed it at the stone, expecting the impact to potentially push him off the small ledge. Instead the door stone shimmered and vanished. Earth temperature air rushed out of a small tunnel to greet Irsu, smelling of stone and time.

He pushed inside and collapsed to his knees on the stone path. He pulled a cord that freed Hobrith, who rolled off Irsu's back onto the floor. Irsu made the stricken warrior as comfortable as possible.

Soon, the seventeen surviving dwarves were in the hall with him, many of them sitting down and leaning on walls as well.

Coragg plopped down next to Irsu. "You should get the key and close the door. It's cold out."

Irsu chuckled as he wearily rose and walked to the door. He listened for a moment as the wind howled past. He thought he could hear voices up above, in the ridiculous language the humans spoke.

Floating in the air, the iron rod, Key to the Lost Hold, was easy to see. If the stone of the door was still present, the rod would be buried in it. Irsu grabbed the key and pulled it to him, inside the hallway. The door, after a half minute pause, solidified back to stone and the noise of wind vanished.

He returned to his spot on the wall. "Done."

"Hobrith is dead."

Irsu grimaced. "Did he—"

"He just passed. You kept your promise." Coragg stood, then extended a hand for Irsu to do the same.

Irsu clasped his friends arm and they embraced, celebrating the completion of the worst of their journey.

"I'm tired. We camp here," Irsu said, settling back down to the floor.

"I extended my hand to help you up. Stand for me," Coragg said.

Irsu did so. Something in his friend's voice said protest wasn't an option.

Coragg leaned forward and put his forehead on Irsu's. "You are the greatest leader I have served with. You upheld dwarven honor, even when we were ordered not to do so. You fought harder when your brother was lost. You gave enemies honorable deaths when they fought with dishonor. You brought us here, to our goal. You are, Irsu Crackstone, *amblu-gane*."

That was a word Irsu wasn't even remotely worthy of. But to discount the use of it by Coragg would be a huge insult. Irsu was conflicted inside.

The soldiers lined up, and one by one they clasped his arms and repeated the phrase. "*Amblu-gane*."

Legendary warrior. The title hadn't been given in centuries, and only the Underking could bestow it. But for his warriors to say it in association with him was the greatest honor he'd ever had. And they knew what he was four years ago. A second son. A child-maker. A hearth-cutter. Certainly no warrior.

"I am not worthy," Irsu said, his internal conflict getting the better of him.

"That is why you are worthy," Coragg replied. "You came from nothing to this. Most train their entire lives. You lived as a hearth maker. Now you are a warrior among warriors. *Amblu-gane.*"

"*Amblu-gane,*" the survivors repeated in unison once more.

"Damn it," Irsu said. "We can't camp now. Let's get to the Great Hall and do what must be done."

Coragg grinned. "As I expected. I will carry Hobrith from here."

Irsu didn't protest. He wasn't sure he could carry himself let alone a dead dwarf. But he'd do it for his soldiers.

Chapter 30 - Flesh Wall

June 2, 1940

It was a good day so far. The Matador's tanks were full, four 25 kilogram bags of French wheat were in the back of the truck, and Wilkes had sacked a small first aid clinic in Neuvilly. All that was missed on the east-west road they'd taken before; these resources were only visible from the north road out of town.

Now they were on the road with bellies full of porridge, cow haunch, and unleavened bread they'd cooked last night. Harry admired the French landscape as the hedges rolled past by the road.

"This land was once British," Miller informed him.

"Get out," Harry said.

"No, really. Back in the days when Kings weren't just fellows in fancy clothes, this territory was controlled by our lot."

"Really?" Tim asked.

"Close to back home as we been in a while then, innit?" Harry said to Tim.

The two senior soldiers laughed, Miller frowned.

"Relax, Miller, we're just looking for a joy where we can find it," Harry told him.

"It's nothing anyway, this place is French as French gets now," Miller said, venom in his voice.

"You don't like the French?" Harry asked.

"Who does?" Tim threw in.

"It was the French who burned the Templars," Miller explained. "Sacked the treasuries, that was the goal. Because some dainty French king couldn't keep his bills paid."

"Ah, and because your great-granddad—"

"Yeah, it's mostly about him," Miller conceded. "But what if the Templars were still around as they once were?" He waved his hand out the front window, through the hole left by the missing panel shot out by a crossbow bolt a week earlier. "All this might not be happening. If anyone would have known how to stop it, it would have been the Templars."

"Harry, you reckon that's right?" Tim asked.

"Kid knows more than I ever will," Harry conceded. "Might be right."

Up ahead movement on the road caught their attention. The somehow disconcerting movement of bodies not fully muscled.

"Damn them," Tim fumed as he braked the lorry. "We were making good time."

"Dead closing in behind. Half a mile away," one of the men yelled from the back.

"Miller, you got a trick?" Harry asked.

"For one of them, maybe two," Miller replied. Harry could see the fear on the young man's face as he tried to stifle it.

"Be right back." Harry climbed out of the cab and stood on top of the lorry. The men in the bed plagued him with questions, but he was busy and waved them off. Raising his glasses, he scoped the north pack. Several dozen yards of writhing skeletons and semi-formed beasts. Same to the south.

The road was out then.

To the west was a small village, it was packed with the dead. Thin feelers of the monstrosities, probably a few yards thick, stretched out from the village to both the north and south packs. Almost like the dead were a single living thing, feeling for food.

He turned around. To the east feelers were moving toward each other from the north and south but hadn't connected yet. He jumped down and dove back into his seat. "East, Tim, and quickly."

Tim plunged the Matador through a hedge into the fields. The going was easier than Harry'd expected, this field wasn't plowed. The farmers must have been chased off before the ground was ready.

Good fortune for Harry's men in the back.

As they drove through the slowly enclosing box, the dead passed by about fifty yards on each side of the lorry. Their hisses and squeals could easily be heard over the Matador's laboring engine.

"Don't fail us now," Harry said, patting the dash.

The smell of the dead was putrid. A mix of fresh blood, bile, and rot.

When they were finally past, Harry ordered a stop a half mile out of the trap. He climbed to the top again.

"A wall stretches north-northwest as far as I can see," he said. "The road is out, we'll never get past them."

"Where to?" Tim called up.

"Northeast. Toward Belgium and Germany."

"Delightful," Tim said as Harry sat back down in his seat. "At least the Krauts won't feast on us, I suppose. Better to be prisoners than dead."

"Speaking of, we haven't seen any Germans for a long time. Where are all the tanks? All their soldiers?"

"No bloody idea," Tim said.

"Withdrawn to choke points would be my guess," Miller said. "Bridges, river crossings, hills with good coverage of the surrounding terrain."

"Now you're a tactician?" Tim mocked.

"No, he's right." Harry shook his head. "We're out here wandering the countryside with the dead setting noose traps for us, and the Germans are securing zones."

"Should we find such a zone?"

"Do you want to be a guest of the Germans?" Harry replied. "Keep going northeast. The plan hasn't changed, we're going to scout that gate and get word to HQ with the wireless."

"It's going to be rough doing," Tim said, not particularly to anyone.

"Grumbling, Tim?"

"Honesty. We'll be lucky to make it."

"Haven't you noticed?" Harry asked. "We're pretty damned lucky. Look at the things we've survived that destroyed entire units around us."

"Then full speed ahead, by all means," Tim laughed. "We're the lucky lot, bastards of the 25th Brigade. Abandoned and left to wander, we'll show them."

"That's the spirit, you sarcastic twit."

"Me? Sarcastic?" Tim asked, mocking indignity. "It's not like we just about died or anything like that."

"Get on with it," Harry laughed, gesturing out the window. "I have a steak to eat with the missus if you'll just drive."

"Are you two married?" Miller asked.

"Do you mean are we married to wives? Or am I married to Tim?" Harry asked.

He and Tim laughed.

Miller's face flushed red. "No, I mean to wives."

"I am," Harry said. "Nobody'll have that one."

"The dead are forming a wall behind us," Hans yelled forward, interrupting their conversation. "Closing it up quick."

Harry looked at Tim, hoping his face didn't look as worried as his friend.

"Stop?" Tim asked.

"For a second." Harry jumped back up on the roof once more. Sure enough, walls were being formed around them, but not to the northeast, at least not like the other three directions. Stragglers marched across the way north, but very few and the large vehicle could easily drive over that many.

Harry jumped back into position. "Go. Straight ahead. No delay." He leaned out the window. "Hang on in back. We're not going to spare the suspension for a mile or two."

The cross country trek was rough. The lorry was built to take much more than the men were. He heard more than one expletive from the back end.

Tim wasted no time. Two of the dead met their end under the lorry's tires, making a splattering noise as their bones crunched into paste.

"We're through that line," Harry said, pleased. "I think we'll see another."

"You a clairvoyant?" Tim asked.

"They're laying traps, can't you see?" Harry explained. "They might even be herding us. Giving us a direction to escape, a single choice that pushes us further—"

"North." Miller said, completing the sentence. "They want us to go to the gate. Just as the red soldiers we met did."

"What do you think will happen if we defy that? Go south instead?"

"We're food for our ancestors," Harry answered. "There might be an overall intelligence herding us north, but in close the dead are nothing but murderous. We can't risk that."

"North it is then," Tim said. "It'd go quicker if they'd get off the road."

"Aye, mate. It would," Harry agreed. "But I doubt anyone's thinking of our comfort but us."

Ahead of them the gate loomed over their spirits, although it didn't look that large from this distance. The skies were clear over France, but in the other world, through the dome over Rotterdam, the skies were dark with storms. Probably rare there from the terrain Harry'd seen when they first discovered the gate over a week ago.

"Scoops," Miller said.

"What?"

"Scoops. The dead are forming scoops across the land, circling the living, then closing their lines to force them toward the gate."

"Seems to be," Harry agreed.

"They're clearing the land," Miller continued. "They want humans to go to their world, they want this one from us."

"Sure," Harry agreed again. "Stating the obvious, preaching to the choir."

Miller was silent for a while. "What's the motive?"

"How would we bloody know that?" Tim asked.

"We saw through the gate when we first looked at it. The other side didn't seem so horrible. And there's magic there, which obviously humans can tap into. So theoretically pushing us through the gate would make us stronger, not more vulnerable."

"That doesn't make any sense now," Harry agreed. "Maybe we're food on the other side, we don't get time to figure things out."

"That's right cheery," Tim said, angry. "What's the point in that?"

"Speculation."

"With all due respect, keep that shite in your own head, not mine."

Harry grinned. "Fine, Tim. I didn't realize you were a lily with a fragile stem."

No answer.

They'd know soon enough what the purpose was, Harry assumed. They were being guided that way. But what the other side didn't know was this time a fully armed British infantry squad was coming through. With no reservations about putting a bullet in anything they didn't like. Add Miller to the equation and they weren't to be trifled with.

"I'm sorry, Tim." Harry reached across Miller and patted his friend's arm. "I'm stressed too. We'll get through. We're the lucky ones, right?"

Tim grinned, clearly in a forgiving mood. "Right."

Chapter 31 - The Great Hall

The procession down the hallway was slow. The records for the way to get into the Lost Hold, other than how to open the door, were destroyed or simply misplaced ages before now. Irsu proceeded with caution, and Numo, being the scout, took the lead.

"I haven't seen a single trap," Numo whispered back to Irsu. "That worries me in itself. It's possible the hold was sacked long ago if the humans found it."

"They didn't find it," Irsu replied, confident. "If they had, there would be trash up and down this corridor. It's how they are."

Numo shrugged and kept pushing forward, slow and steady.

The path wasn't short. The corridor wound down through the mountain in a sequence of precise turns equal to one sixth of a circle. Always with a consistent downward slope.

"You think we're under the mean ground level for this area?" Coragg asked.

Irsu shrugged. "I don't know. I hope there are plenty of charts and plans locked away here to explain the layout to us. If not we'll spend two years looking for booby traps and mapping the place."

As Irsu stepped forward something clicked under his feet. He closed his eyes and said a prayer to Mordain. "Numo. I think I'm on a trap."

Numo stopped and returned to the spot. "Give me the lantern," he said to Coragg.

The scout swept the lantern in a circle around Irsu, carefully studying the floor. "Plate trap. One subsurface conduit out from the plate, you probably activated a trigger stepping on the thing. Once you step off, the trap will rebound, pulling the trigger and releasing whatever effect it's designed to kill with."

"Can you fix it, or do I have to grow old in this spot?" Irsu growled, irritated he was the one who found the trap.

"I can fix it. See the slight difference in the stone color along this line? That's where the conduit runs. The grout has changed colors over the many years, just enough for me to see it."

"Why didn't you see it when you passed over it?" Coragg demanded.

"I didn't have this fancy lantern of yours," Numo replied. "When I asked for it back up top, you said no, said I'd need my hands free."

Irsu chuckled. "You did say that, Coragg."

"I thought he would," the warrior complained. "We all thought there'd be traps every twenty steps."

"More like every two thousand steps," Numo said, "but since you're an expert in my job I'm sure you'll know I'm about to ask you for your dagger."

Coragg sighed as he handed it over. "What for?"

Numo stabbed the tip into the grout, flaking a piece off. "Good, they used the cheap stuff. I can scrape it out and get to the line."

Irsu looked at Coragg as Numo dragged the blade through the abrasive seal over the conduit. "You're going to need a new dagger."

"Aye, what's new."

It took Numo half an hour, but he finally reached the passage under the rock surface that contained the wire for the trap. He drove a stone biting nail into the floor and carefully, without pulling the wire back toward Irsu, tied it off to the nail.

"It'll have to be disarmed later. It's a hazard, but it's inert for the moment," Numo reported.

"I'll stay here until the last of us are past," Coragg said. "To make sure none of these oafs kick the trap loose and set it off. Then I'll make my way back forward." He handed Numo the lamp. "You take this."

"Aye," Numo said, not making much of Coragg's change of heart.

Irsu lifted his foot from the plate, which snapped back upward level with the stone floor. Nothing happened, it was successfully deactivated for the moment. "Onward."

It took the procession a day, and over two dozen more traps, to reach the archway into the great hall of the Lost Hold.

Irsu was first to step into the wide expanse of floor. The ceiling disappeared into the darkness above. The columns that marked the main procession disappeared into the distance ahead of him.

This place was big. Bigger than Iron Mountain Hold. By far.

Irsu didn't really know which way to go, but the results would probably be the same whichever way he picked. He gestured to the right, feeling in his gut that they'd come to the main gateway of the hold on that path. Did he know? No. But it felt correct somehow. "Alright, we're going to try and not get ourselves killed. So we'll walk to the front gate alone the wall, then down the procession toward the public throne. There we might find some answers about our next steps."

The remnants of Iron Company followed Irsu around the room, into the darkness. Their torches fluttered as each burned out in turn. After what seemed like an eternity of mystery and fear, the front gate loomed before them. To the left the procession led toward what he hoped was the public throne.

In the distance clanking echoed through the halls. A strange whirring sound as well.

Whirrr. Clank. Whirrr. Clank.

"What's that," Coragg whispered.

Irsu shrugged. He had an idea, but he didn't know for sure. Whatever it was, machinery of some kind operated after thousands of years under Nollen. The sounds were a testament to the durability of Dwarven engineering, although also another source of fear. The only reason to have a machine working at this point, and over all those years between, would be if it was needed to protect or maintain something. "My guess is a Guardian."

"We can't fight a Guardian," Coragg hissed. "We're dead if that's the case."

"Maybe it isn't here to fight dwarves," he replied. "We won't know until we get to the public throne. It's also possible the controls for it are located there."

"Then we should run," Numo urged him. "If it's a Guardian, it knows we're here."

Irsu grunted his agreement, then sighed deeply. He was tired, worn down, and sick of being tested. "To the throne," he yelled. The sound echoed back to him from a dozen angles.

His remaining warriors raced down the length of the Great Hall. The slap of their boots reverberated into the darkness. Their breathing became labored, and heavy weapons became as lead in their hands.

An indeterminate time later they reached the throne. A series of circular platforms, growing ever smaller, rose from the floor. At the top a throne, tarnished with the ages, stood over them. Dwarves fell about the steps, trying to regain their composure.

Whirrr. Clank. Whirrr. Clank.

The sound was still growing louder.

"The throne," Coragg said, winded.

Irsu climbed. The front of the platform had steps rising through the circular disks toward the top. Probably fifty or more. Irsu placed one foot forward and above the other, over and over again. He was unnaturally tired. Each step became harder than the one before it.

"A trap," Numo huffed from below. "It's draining us."

Irsu saw it now. Green sigils alongside the steps flared for a moment, just barely bright enough to see, then dropped back into invisibility. Each time they flared, Irsu was a little more tired. They'd drain him of his ability to move, then when he lay on the steps exhausted, they'd drain him of his life.

He'd heard of such things. Dwarven priest magic.

"I am a dwarf," he bellowed, finding energy he didn't know he had. "I will not be denied now."

He stepped again and again, higher up the dais. By the top he was reduced to crawling, but the last step finally appeared before him.

Ahead of him the throne, embedded with jewels and cast of silver, waited.

He dragged himself the distance to the chair, then heaved himself off the ground. It felt like his joints were tearing apart. His breathing took more effort than cutting his hearth back home ever had.

He raised himself to stand, both of his hands grasping the arms of the throne. One of his elbows failed, spinning him around. His butt plopped into the seat of the throne purely by happenstance. Bone crushingly tired from his efforts, he closed his eyes, ready to die.

"Centuries, then millennia have passed. I have waited," a deep voice boomed from the darkness.

The Guardian.

Irsu tried to find the energy to search for a secret compartment, something that might contain a control gem for the golem he feared.

A great monstrosity appeared out of the darkness. Its face was a circular cavern of grinding teeth, ready to shred the enemies of the dwarven race. Or a dwarf unlucky enough to find himself abandoned without a control gem.

A voice boomed into the darkness. "Only a dwarf can make the ascent to the throne. Only my creators have that level of vitality. Only a great warrior among dwarves has the will to make the climb."

The Guardian back at Iron Mountain never spoke. This one didn't shut up.

"Kill us already, if that is your task," Irsu said. "I have no will left, warrior or not."

"No, no need for that," one of the men below said. "We're fine."

Irsu tried not to laugh, but a chuckle rose in his gut. Finally, a laugh erupted and filled the hall. He wondered where he'd found the energy.

"Only soldiers of Iron laugh at death," the Guardian said. "I do not kill my creators. I serve them."

Irsu felt his life returning, a tiny sip at a time. Several minutes passed as he recovered. When he felt well enough, he grabbed his axe and stood at the edge of the platform's top circle. That put him level with the face of the Guardian, who stood on the floor half a kadros distant.

"I yield this hold to you, Warrior," the golem said in its booming voice. "I now protect this hold for you."

Sporadic laughter started among the men. They rose up in a great cheer, their lethargy also abated.

"*Amblu-gane!*"

"Hush," Irsu told them.

"Even the Guardian sees it," another dwarf said.

"HUSH!" Irsu bellowed. His voice echoed back and forth among the pillars, seeming to come from a thousand directions. He sort of liked the effect. It gave his tone more authority.

The men slowly grew quiet.

"Silence," he urged. "We are not done. We must find and open the way home."

Cheers erupted again. The warriors knew they were almost finished. Just one final step remained, and glory would find them. Beer. And rest. And maybe a lass or two.

"We have secured the hold, and the Guardian has recognized us," Irsu ordered after waiting for them to settle down one more time.

"Now we find the temple of Mordain. I believe it is there we will find what we need."

The Guardian turned away and marched toward the front gate. It finally had something to protect, warriors to watch over. It would assume the post Guardians historically held, instead of wandering an empty hold.

Irsu grinned. He started to tell himself that he was glad the Guardian was an easy conquest. But it wasn't. He thought of the last few steps to the public throne, and the agony of lifting himself to sit.

No. Like every other step he'd taken toward Nollen and the Lost Hold, that one had been insanely difficult. Just a different type of struggle.

He started down the steps. There couldn't be more than just a few struggles left.

Chapter 32 - Crossed

June 3, 1940

There was no mistaking the intent of the dead now. Driven by unknown forces, they were formed into fenced boxes across much of northern France, from what Harry could tell. At their lunch break, when they stopped to get some fuel from an abandoned French tank, Miller was on the wireless. When he'd raised the German garrison at Valenciennes, the garrison explained their situation.

Walled in by the dead on all sides.

"Is the barrier toward Rotterdam less robust?" Harry'd asked a German who spoke English.

"Yah, if we wanted to break out, that'd be the way," was the answer.

He left Miller to get news from the Germans, so he could confirm his suspicions to Timothy. "It's not just us they're herding through the gate. It's everyone."

"Why in blazes would they?" Tim pondered.

"We'll find out soon enough. If we resist at this point, we're food for dead men. If we cooperate, we're going through."

"It'll be dark soon." We've got enough diesel to get to the gate, but probably not much beyond that," Wilkes said.

"We should get some distance from those blokes," Tim waved toward the wall of dead to the east, "and stop to fuel up. We need at least ten minutes to discuss what's happening with the men. They deserve to know."

"They know," Wilkes said, shrugging. "What they deserve to know is a plan for when we go through. Although we get it that we don't know what the other side holds. But ready guns, or something like that would be nice to hear. Leadership is important."

"We'll try to have a talk before we cross over, Wilkes," Harry offered. "For now, we look for a fuel stop on our way. More food would be good. This wheat won't last forever."

Back on the road they continued north.

A farm that was their salvation. A pair of fuel tanks raised above the ground had plenty of fuel in them. Diesel and petrol. High on a platform, the tanks were set up to gravity feed fuel into tractors.

"Not a tractor in sight," Miller said. "You think they fled on those?"

"Beats walking," Jones answered.

"Check the house," Tim ordered the men. "Get every scrap of food and bring me any cotton you find along with any empty bottles."

"You're making petrol bombs?" Miller asked.

"You have a better idea?" Tim asked him.

"No, it's a splendid idea, actually. It will work well with my trick."

Harry nodded. Petrol bombs worked well enough on their own normally, but with Miller around they wouldn't even need to light them before throwing at a target.

"Sack the house," Harry ordered. "Forks, spoons, linen, bedding, towels, metal dishes, cups. If it looks useful, bring it, we'll pack the lorry as full as we can. We have no idea where we're going to wind up."

The men rushed to the task. Soon the sounds of haste with the edge of panic erupted from inside the farmhouse.

Harry looked over the Matador while Wilkes fueled it. Garrett found bottles in the barn, apparently for storing animal milk. The lids on them sealed well. As the wall of dead slid closer from the south, Tim filled bottles with petrol until the last minute. When he was done, almost thirty of the quart bottles rode in a basket in back, full of fuel, cushioned by pillows from the bedrooms. Sheets and towels torn into thin strips provided the linen for fuses.

It had taken them twenty minutes to fuel. The lorry was running well, and everything looked good. They were as ready as they were going to get. Thanks to the farmers who'd fled the Germans, Harry's squad had full tanks on both sides of the Matador, and four Jerry cans full of diesel as well.

The men loaded back into the truck with some food that was starting to show its age, petrol bombs, and plenty of bedding.

"Why bedding?" Wilkes asked.

"Do you like sleeping on the ground?" Harry'd asked him. When the private shook his head, Harry grinned. "Me either. We don't know what's on the other side."

"Everyone on?" Tim yelled out the window toward the back.

The whistles and groans of the dead were audible now, and the first of them were starting to appear from around the corners of the house.

"They'd best be," Harry replied.

"We're off."

The farm was on a road that cut east a bit, then back north. The dead left the road open, so they took it. They were faster, and the ride was smoother as a result. Two hours past that they'd driven into Belgium and the gate was prominent in the sky ahead. They'd looted a few more buildings when they'd had time, securing more assets for the crossing.

An inverted dome that looked different from the surrounding sky was to the north now. While it was cloudy over the road they were on, the clouds disappeared where Earth's reality ended and the other side began. On the other side, in a different world or existence, a vibrant blue expanse seemed to stretch into infinity.

"Least it's not storming over there anymore," Harry said.

Nobody answered him. The sight of what awaited bore down on them, not only physically in that it towered higher and higher above them, but in their morale. Harry knew fear was eating at every one of his men. Maybe going through the barrier would simply kill them.

Maybe they'd find themselves on another world. Maybe once they crossed they'd see Rotterdam.

It was the not knowing that was tough. Maybe they should have kept going south when the way was clear. That wasn't a choice now. Whatever happened, it was Harry's doing. He'd decided, because he was the officer. Their fates were on his conscience.

As they pulled up to the edge of the barrier, they could see the energy that kept the gate open playing along the surface.

They disembarked and examined it. Above them a bird flew through as it was chased by a hawk, in a desperate bid to escape being the hawk's dinner.

"Feels a bit like that," Wilkes said, his voice emotionless.

"Yes, I suppose it does," Harry admitted. "I'm sorry it's come to this, but if we're to continue to exist, the way is clear. We go in."

"Or die here," Miller added, gesturing toward the south.

The first of the dead were breaking through the tree line and moving toward them. He only saw a few at the moment, but soon there would be more.

"Everyone's gun fully loaded?" Tim asked the team.

Nods all around. If they went down, it wouldn't be without a fight.

"Garrett, you and Jone... okay, not Jones, his throwing arm is off. Henry, you're with Garrett. Be ready to use those Molotov cocktails we made if it comes to that."

"I don't see anything on the other side that threatens us," Jones said. "It's just… dirt and scrub. Not that I can see it very well with the distortion."

"As Harry so kindly pointed out to me, people going through might be like ringing the dinner bell. If we're to be food for monsters, let's not make it a free meal," Tim responded.

Everyone laughed the uneasy laugh of men who might be in their last minutes.

Garrett, using his pistol to save rifle ammo, shot the first of the dead to arrive through the head, it fell to the ground in a mass that quivered as if it might heal itself, rise back up, and come after them again. The next of the dead was a few minutes away.

"I think they're drawing their energy from in there," Miller speculated, gesturing toward the gate. "We're the underdogs here, and we might not be able to kill them at all."

As if to emphasize his point, the WWI soldier Garrett shot was trying to rise once more.

"Then let's get on with it," Harry ordered. "On the lorry. Now. We're going."

Tim started the diesel, which for some reason comforted Harry. The reliable motor of the Matador had seen them through confrontations with the dead of their world and the living from another.

"Damn," Tim said as he engaged the clutch.

They drove forward. Toward destinations unknown.

Chapter 33 - Berlin

June 3, 1940

"I now pronounce you man and wife," the chaplain said. "Heil, von Krosigk."

"Heil, von Krosigk," Ernst and Herta repeated in unison.

The chaplain turned back to his desk, sat down, and for all appearances immediately forgot that Ernst and his new bride were even present.

They kissed deeply, surely that was the proper thing for the moment, and then looked toward the man who joined them together one last time.

"*Danke, Kaplan*,"

"Yah, yah," the man replied, waving them toward the door.

As they exited the administrative office, a car was waiting. It would take them to the Berlin airport. Three JU-52s waited to transport the newly married couple, the research team, and two dozen SS troops to Ethiopia.

Rain poured from a sodden sky, drenching the world with tears. Nature herself wept for the great hole torn into her side at Rotterdam. He shielded Herta with the umbrella he'd had the foresight to bring, then opened the door for his new bride.

"Will it always be this way?" she asked him.

"For you?" he laughed. "Yes, dear Herta. I finally found you, I'm not about to let you escape me because of my neglect."

He joined her in the back seat from the other side. The car pulled away from the curb, the flags fluttering from the front fenders told everyone on the streets that important people were being taken somewhere.

"We're finally off," Herta said, smiling as broad as Ernst had ever seen. "Honeymooning in Ethiopia and securing the greatest artifact in history for the Reich."

"I have asked that Italian troops already near our destination be made available for our use if we need them," Ernst told her. "Whether they are or not will be another question that we'll answer later."

"Undependable and lazy, the Italians," Herta said. "I was shocked when Herr Hitler allied himself with them."

Ernst put his arm around her and pulled her close, conscious of the driver in the front seat. "Great men can make mistakes. There is no doubt. And we can speak of Hitler's as having made a few, now.

But remember to always think before you speak of our living heroes." He kissed her forehead. "Trust me, I've seen the price demanded if they even think you might be disloyal. I have proved that I am not."

"Something you would tell me?" she asked, concerned.

"It was nothing," he assured her. "What is important is that we support von Krosigk. He is, as our new Führer, bound for greatness. And he is taking Germany and us along with him."

"Heil, von Krosigk," she said, kissing his cheek.

"Heil, von Krosigk," the driver repeated, which Ernst quickly parroted.

That confirmed the driver was listening to them.

They pulled up next to the Junkers on the tarmac shortly thereafter. Men were loading crates onto each of the planes, while the SS soldiers stood in a formation in front of the one they'd be in. An officer of the SS stood in front of them, giving the soldiers direction and guidance for what he thought the mission was.

After Ernst exited the car and once again endured the rain so Herta could stay dry under his umbrella, they both walked to the officer.

Ernst extended his hand. "Ernst Haufmann, Ahnenerbe Director."

"You are the man this is all about," the officer replied. "Congratulations on your selection as Director, Herr Haufmann. I am Obersturmführer Werner von Krosigk, at your service, Director."

"You are related—"

"— to the Führer, yes. He is my father, although I am a bastard son."

Herta laughed, surprising Ernst. "You're a Waffen-SS soldier about to undertake one of the greatest journeys in the history of the Reich, to secure an artifact that will cement the Reich's power, and you're whining that you're a bastard?"

Ernst handed her the umbrella. "Get to the plane. Now." He pointed at the center aircraft of the three. "That one is ours."

She looked at him, shocked, then hurt. But did as he said.

After she was gone he looked at the SS Officer. "I apologize for that. She is enamored with the romance of the journey we are making."

"What she said, is this true? Is it that important."

"It is... may I call you Werner?"

The young officer nodded.

"It is, Werner. Do you need to fly with your soldiers, or can you fly in my aircraft so I can properly brief you on the mission?"

Werner turned to his soldiers. "Grab your things. Board the aircraft. I am riding with the Director, in order that he might brief me and we can protect him better. Heil, von Krosigk."

"Heil, von Krosigk," the soldiers repeated in unison with the straight armed salute that went with it.

The men grabbed their things and ran to their aircraft as the engines started turning over. The dark clouds overhead and the rain pouring down made the scene seem surreal to Ernst. Behind the third plane a bus pulled up with Ernst's research team. Workers disembarked the vehicle to unload the research supplies.

"Does that phrase ever seem self serving for you now?" Ernst asked Werner.

"Heil, von Krosigk?" The young officer laughed. "I am going to like working with you, Director. It seems you're aware of, and care about knowing those around you."

"When they are worthy," Ernst said, putting his arm around the man. "That is how life works. The strong rule the weak. We, Werner, are the strong."

Let him think that they were friends. Another soul who felt Ernst was a man who cared. Ernst did care. About three things.

Himself, Germany, and Herta.

In precisely that order.

He walked up the steps to the trimotor with the officer in tow.

Chapter 34 - *Amblu-Gane*

The temple of Mordain was at the center of the hold, just as expected. It lay under the rooms that comprised the Underking's residence, not that a king occupied the structure. Stone steps outside the residential rooms allowed the common dwarves access to worship at the temple.

Irsu stood at the head of the stairs, looking down at the golden doors with Mordain's twisting symbol.

"I'm glad we didn't have to destroy the Guardian," Coragg said. "Now if the humans ever break into this place, they'll be in for a real surprise. I'd have hated to leave it defenseless against them."

Irsu looked at Coragg, incredulous. Then he started laughing. The laugh grew, until it was a belly laugh so deep he had to sit down on the steps. The other dwarves started laughing with him, uncertain as to why.

"What's so funny?" Coragg said, wiping a tear. "Don't you feel the same?"

"Oh, I do," Irsu said between his outbreaks of mirth. "What's funny is you think we," he waved at the half dead squad around him, "could beat a Guardian."

"It could have happened," Coragg said with crossed arms, his laughter ended.

Irsu laughed harder. "Coragg, stop! I might pee myself."

Coragg was silent and simply stared. Under that stern gaze, the mirth came to an end.

Irsu stood and looked at the doors. It felt good to enjoy the company of his soldiers before what was probably the final trial that awaited them.

"Here we go," he said. "If there isn't a way to open the gate in here, then we're probably going to starve before we find it."

"This place is huge," one of the dwarves agreed.

A few steps downward and a small landing later, the handles for the great gold doors loomed large in Irsu's face.

"Here goes," he grunted as he grabbed one, expecting to have to wrestle it open.

Instead the door opened with ease, and Irsu almost fell down. The dwarven engineering, ten thousand years on, worked perfectly and the door, heavier than a war wagon, glided on its hinges.

Inside lights, dormant for many lifetimes, sprang into existence and illuminated a stunning room. Dwarven priestly magic, long inert on Earth, reasserted itself into the world of the humans.

Still, it was magic, and words of unease passed between the soldiers.

Irsu, on edge, knew he had to go in first.

Crossing the threshold felt like the bravest thing he'd ever done. The hair on the back of his neck stood up.

With reason.

The room was two hundred cubic *horats* of hollow space. More steps led down to the main floor of the temple. At the center a dry fountain, with a carved image of Mordain's two manifestations, rose upward toward the ceiling. A platform, from which priests would give sermons, circled the fountain a few feet above the lowest point of the temple. Stone bleachers circled that platform after a small expanse of flat floor.

Gold and jewels glistened in the light from the glow globes floating below the ceiling. Along the wall were recesses. Irsu recognized it, the wall was a crypt wall, where notable dead would rest for a while before being burned, so family and admirers could pay last respects and celebrate the life of a hero. The sanctified ground would prevent the dead from returning to life in most cases.

But apparently not in this case.

Three of the crypts were inhabited. Three armored and armed dwarven corpses crawled out of their holes on the far side of the room.

"Skuldors," Coragg said.

"What?"

"Crypt guardians. Soldiers who voluntarily stay past death to serve. They protect this place. We're in for it."

"Great," Irsu sighed. "That means a lot since you think we could take the Guardian." He turned to his troops. "The unwounded fight these abominations. Three squads of at least four, one on each of the… what are they again?"

"Skuldors," Coragg replied.

"Skuldors," Irsu repeated. "Have at them!"

The dwarves charged down the bleachers, toward the other side of the room. The skuldors did the same, with a lot less noise. The two sides met on the level floor between the platform and the bleachers.

Irsu's first impression was that the things looked fragile. The armor, which probably fit fine in life, rattled against desiccated skin and bones. The weapons of the skuldors, two axes and an ancient kopesh, caused dust to fall from the hands of the guardians with each twist or movement. All three bore shields as well.

His first impression was the wrong impression.

Irsu's group fought the kopesh guardian, who's first act was to slip nimbly downward and hack at Irsu's feet. That forced him to jump, and as he did the creature's shield arm hammered him with the flat of the shield. Irsu was knocked down and slid a good distance back, stopped by the rise of the first bleacher.

Stars flashed in front of him, and he wondered how the breastplate of his armor wasn't flat now.

Good stuff, dwarven armor. And his was some of the best.

He jumped up despite wanting to lay there, and then surged back into the fight. The creature was brutalizing Coragg and two of the soldiers. Two soldiers in other squads were already on the ground.

Numo was off doing something unrelated to the combat near the center of the room, standing still as weapons flashed nearby.

"Numo, get your blade swinging," Irsu ordered.

The scout was reading something written on the base of the fountain. This was not the time for the strange dwarf to satisfy curious urges.

The creature facing Irsu's team of four swiveled to face Irsu just as he arrived back into the combat. It must have sensed Irsu's threat magically because any eyes it once had were long gone.

Irsu raised his own shield and swung his axe in an overhead swing, the blade cracked down against the creature. As he did so the creature thrust forward with its kopesh, a move Irsu blocked with his shield.

Or so he thought.

The kopesh's tip, surprisingly sharp and strong after so long in darkness, pierced the shield and tore into Irsu's arm. The blade went through leather and skin, deep into muscle. Warm blood welled up from his body, spilling onto the floor.

"NO!" Coragg yelled, looking into Irsu's face.

Coragg attacked with new ferocity.

The creature pulled on the sword embedded in Irsu's shield, trying to block the attacks of the battle raging dwarf. It succeeded in jerking Irsu forward, but not in releasing the weapon from Irsu's shield.

As the room's lights dimmed around him, he saw the creature's head come off. Thanks to Coragg's blade.

Irsu fell to the floor. His arm was opened from wrist to shoulder, and he was losing blood fast. The remains of the creature fell on top of his legs, Coragg quickly brushed them aside.

Under the stones platform Numo was dragging his finger along some script and holding a water skin. Whatever madness lived in the mind of the scout didn't matter much to Irsu any longer.

He wanted to go out with his friend smiling. "You're right, Coragg," Irsu said.

"About what, *Amblu-gane*?"

"You could have taken the Guardian."

Coragg laughed, tears fell from his big nose onto Irsu's cheek. "You're not done yet, damn you."

The last thing Irsu saw clearly was the scout climbing the statue as one of the creatures, apparently having taken down the warriors fighting it, tried to grab at Numo's feet and drag the mad dwarf back down to his doom.

Irsu couldn't move his body, but he used his now failing eyes to point in the direction of the fight. "You're not done protecting our people yet, Coragg. My friend."

Coragg nodded, stood up, wiped his tears and surged toward the enemy once more.

Irsu embraced the darkness as it came for him, his friend being the last vision to fill his mind.

<<<<TO BE CONTINUED>>>>

Glossary:

Harry's squad:

1. Harry Hughes: Lieutenant, light machine gunner, platoon leader

2. Timothy Martin: Corporal, light machine gun crew, 2nd in command.

3. John Miller: Private, Radioman, descendant of a Templar Knight

4. Geoffrey Wilkes: Private, Rifleman, Stubborn but intelligent. Crack shot.

5. Benjamin Garrett: Private, Rifleman

6. Mark Jenkins: Private, Rifleman

7. Thomas Parker: Private, Rifleman

8. David Zimmerman: Private, Rifleman (not mentioned in this book)

9. Lars Henry: Private, Rifleman, hard to understand due to Scottish accent.

10. Michael Aaron: Private, Rifleman (not mentioned in this book)

11. Derek Moore: Private, Rifleman (not mentioned in this book)

12. Unnamed: Killed in Chapter 5 by dwarves

13. Unnamed: Killed in Chapter 5 by dwarves

14. <x> Harris: Killed in Chapter 5 by dwarves

15. <x> Mattison: Killed in Chapter 5 by dwarves

Iron Company: 168 dwarven warriors

Commander: Captain of the Iron Bordnu Crackstone.

Successor: Iron Commander Irsu Crackstone

4 platoons, 40 dwarves each plus 2 leaders:

- Hearthfire Platoon: led by Irsu, then Coragg.

- Anvil Platoon: leader unnamed (now dead)

- Granite Platoon: leader unnamed (now dead)

- Iron Platoon: leader Bordnu (now dead)

Terms and WWII equipment:

- Ahnenerbe – German program to utilize the occult to increase the power of the Reich. This really did exist.

- AP Round – Armor piercing round, bullet with a core designed to penetrate plates of metal.

- Panzer – German Tank. In 1940 German tanks were superior to most other nations, with the exception of the British. Despite the near invincibility of the Matilda II at the time, British tanks were too few and incorrectly utilized to counter the German flood into France.

- Matador Lorry (Truck): A diesel three ton troop transport of British design and manufacture. It had great ground clearance and was quite robust.

- Lorry: What the British still call a truck. If it's a truck that pulls a trailer, it's an articulated lorry.

- Henschel HS-130: An experimental aircraft designed for reconnaissance and bombing from high altitude. It could carry a high tech camera package in the bomb bay instead of bombs. Only a few were made due to design flaws and breakdowns.

- Karabiner 98K: German infantry rifle at the start of WWII. It had great range, was accurate, and fired a large round. It was superior to both British and French rifles in the early war.

- Lee-Enfield: British infantry rifle. It was a good rifle, but inferior to Germany's infantry weapons.

- MAS-36: This French rifle was a reliable weapon, but inferior to the Kar98K. It was actually still scarce at the start of WWII, despite being a 30 year old design. The MAS-36 interestingly had no safety to prevent accidental discharge.

A note on smoking: In the 1940's and earlier cigarette smoking was thought not only to be harmless, but potentially healthy. We later learned that was not the case, and cigarette companies knew that smoking was harmful long before they told us. Smoking (I am an ex-smoker) is harmful, dangerous, and proven to increase the risk of cancer, emphysema, and COPD among other illnesses. Harry doesn't know that. He will probably die later in life of cancer if a bullet doesn't get him first.

Author's note:

Thank you so much for reading my book. If you enjoyed it I would love to get your review on Amazon or Goodreads. Or even if you didn't enjoy it, I would love to know why.

You can reach my author email at: author@damonalan.com

My blog is at www.damonalan.com

And you're welcome to follow or friend me on Facebook, Damon

Alan, anytime. Be warned I say outrageous things on there sometimes just to see how people react. A guy's got to get his entertainment somewhere.

The plan for this book is to make a series, each book covering a few weeks to a month of the WWII time period. Of course it won't follow history as we know it, dragons, elves, dwarves, and the undead tend to change our plans a bit. But I'll be utilizing the technology curve of WWII, the equipment, and the attitudes for the most part. Alongside the standard components of many fantasy worlds. Spitfires, Messerschmitts, and Dragons, Oh my!

If you like space opera, I have several of those written in a series as well. Feel free to check out the adventures of Sarah Dayson as she struggles to save the galaxy.

https://www.amazon.com/gp/product/B077DC96V8

Thanks again, and keep your axes high.

Damon Alan

Printed in Poland
by Amazon Fulfillment
Poland Sp. z o.o., Wrocław

60635403R00162